## "Would yo

Troy McKnigh                                    d
asked the qu                                    g
around her ne~~ck, dangling~~             a
flowery print dress, she looked out of place in
the trendy San Francisco bar. Her wide blue
eyes and heart-shaped face were attractive in a
flower child sort of way. Freckles dotted her
nose and she wore no makeup. Not *exactly* the
type of fiancée he was hoping to find
someday...

**Dear Reader**

When my husband—then boyfriend—and I started dating, we lived a few blocks apart in San Francisco's Marina District. From walking across the Golden Gate Bridge to eating at the many restaurants on Chestnut Street, our dating revolved around life in the city. San Francisco and romance became synonymous, especially after my husband proposed one chilly December night at Crissy Field, with the Golden Gate Bridge as the backdrop.

Four months after we married, we moved and adjusted to life in the suburbs. When it came time to pick the setting for Cassandra and Troy's story, the choice was easy: San Francisco—one of the most romantic cities on Earth. I missed living there so much. I had such wonderful memories of dating, planning our wedding, registering for gifts, being newlyweds. I knew it was the perfect place for my characters to fall in love. I hope you'll agree!

People might sing of leaving their hearts in San Francisco, but it's where I found mine. So did Cassandra and Troy. Enjoy.

*Melissa McClone*

P.S. I love to hear from readers. Please write to me at P.O. Box 63, Lake Oswego, OR 97034, USA.

# FIANCÉ FOR
# THE NIGHT

BY
## MELISSA McCLONE

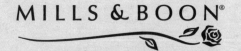

To my husband, Tom, for believing in dreams and believing in me.

*First published in Great Britain 2000
Harlequin Mills & Boon Limited,
Eton House, 18-24 Paradise Road, Richmond, Surrey TW9 1SR*

© Melissa Martinez McClone 1999

ISBN 0 263 81986 8

*Set in Times Roman 10½ on 12 pt.
01-0005-44373*

*Printed and bound in Spain
by Litografia Rosés, S.A., Barcelona*

# 1

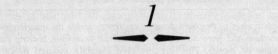

"**W**ould you be my fiancé?"

Troy McKnight stared at the woman who had asked the question. With crystals hanging around her neck, dangling silver earrings and a flowery print dress on, she looked out of place in the trendy San Francisco microbrewery. Her wide, blue eyes and heart-shaped face were attractive in a Haight-Ashbury, flower child sort of way. Freckles dotted her nose, and she wore no makeup. Not exactly the type of fiancée he was hoping to find someday.

He knew nothing about her, not even her name. She'd come up to him, said hello and asked her question. A question he barely heard over the din of the bar crowd. He didn't know if the woman had been serious or if he'd drunk one beer too many. He only remembered ordering one—the half-filled cold glass he held in his hand. "Excuse me, but what did you say?"

Releasing a sigh, she brushed her long, wavy blond hair behind her shoulder. "Would you be my fiancé? Just for tonight, of course."

She said it so matter-of-factly her proposition sounded almost logical. At least he knew it wasn't the beer; he'd heard her right the first time.

Troy took a swig, savoring the cool liquid as it ran down his throat. After a rough day at the office, all he wanted was a drink and another quiet evening at home, nothing else.

Hell, she hadn't introduced herself. She could be a scam artist, a she-devil in disguise, and he the target. Even without lipstick, her full lips were luscious enough to seduce unknowing prey. Troy set his glass on the bar. "Why do you need a fiancé for tonight?"

"It's a long story." She reached for his hand, pushed back the arm of his suit and read the time on his Rolex. Her sunshine and sunflower scent cut through the beer and smoke stench of the brewery. "I don't have time to explain."

"You're asking for a lot without providing any explanation."

She rolled her eyes. "I got myself into a jam with my family. It's only one dinner. My father will pay, so it won't cost you a penny."

Troy hesitated, unsure if he bought her explanation. The woman was attractive enough; she would have no problem finding a real fiancé.

"Look, will you be my fiancé or not?" The edges of her mouth turned up slightly. "I hate to be impatient, but if you say no, I have to find someone else."

She glanced around the bar as if she were looking for her next target. In the jam-packed brewery, she could easily find someone else. Men with rolled-up sleeves and loosened ties stood at nearby tables, relaxing after long hours at the office. Flattered she'd picked him over all the others, his ego swelled. Was he her first choice? He didn't know, and he wondered why the thought bothered him.

Troy didn't know why he was considering posing

as her fiancé. The woman had appeared out of nowhere, yet he couldn't deny his curiosity about her
and her strange proposition. The concern and sense of
urgency in her eyes rang true, but he never took risks.
Spontaneity wasn't part of his plan.

Staring at him, she waited for his answer by tapping
her unpainted fingernails against the oak bar.

If he said no, she seemed to have no qualms about
asking another man to be her fiancé for the night. He
doubted she was a con artist. She looked too much
like an innocent love child with a hint of vulnerability
in her eyes. In a meat market like this, a veritable
smorgasbord of male testosterone, she could end up
with anyone.

At least she would be safe with him.

"This is important to you, isn't it?"

As she tilted her chin, her earrings chimed. "Yes."

A free dinner, an attractive woman. It almost
sounded too easy. Troy thought of Judy White, who
worked in the office next to his. Now she was his type.
He'd seen Judy's fiancé pick her up this afternoon.
For three years, Troy had wanted to ask her out, but
he'd been too busy working to take the time. Now she
was engaged to someone else, and he was sitting in a
bar with a total stranger. What the hell, maybe he
needed a little adventure in his life. "Okay."

She threw her arms around him and kissed his
cheek. "Oh, thank you."

Her impulsiveness surprised him. Troy noticed the
envious glances of other men in the bar. Maybe this
wasn't such a bad idea after all.

Grabbing his arm, she pulled him off his bar stool.
"Come on, we're going to be late."

So fast? What had he gotten himself into? Troy hesitated, unsure if he wanted to experience an adventure tonight. "I need to pay for my beer, first."

Before Troy could reach his wallet, she opened her purse, a multicolored cloth pouch with drawstrings, and pulled out a five-dollar bill. "Will this cover it?"

"Yes." A woman paying? A first for him.

She tossed the money on the bar. "Is there anything else?"

He wanted to say yes. Stop. "No."

"Let's go." She led him out the double glass doors.

A cool breeze blew off the San Francisco Bay. Cars sped by on the Embarcadero. To his right, the lights on the double-decker Bay Bridge twinkled in the evening sky. The pleasant autumn weather was a refreshing change from a day spent in a skyscraper.

"Do you have a car?" she asked.

"Not with me."

She rubbed her temples. "We'll have to take a taxi."

"Where are we—"

"I'll explain everything in a minute." She flagged down a yellow cab. "Stars, please."

Troy followed her into the cab. Stars…he would be getting a good dinner tonight. The restaurant was one of the best in the city, known for creating mouthwatering dishes and attracting a crowd of see-and-be-seen patrons.

As the cab pulled away from the curb, she laughed. "I'm going to pull this off."

He watched her for a moment. Her unrestrained joy, her boundless energy captivated him. He'd never met anyone like her.

She wet her lower lip. "I don't know your name."

"Troy McKnight."

"Troy McKnight." She repeated his name twice. "I like it. Well, Troy. I hope you don't mind me calling you that? After all, we are engaged."

The cabdriver coughed, and Troy ignored him. "Would you mind telling me your name?"

"I'm Cassandra."

Such a serious and formal name for such a lighthearted person. The name Cassie fit her personality much better. "Cassandra what?"

"Oh sorry, I usually go by my first name. Daniels, Cassandra Daniels." She took a deep breath. "I can't believe I found you, and you said yes."

"Why do you need a fiancé?"

She hesitated, drawing her honey gold eyebrows together.

"I need to know what's going on, otherwise…"

"You're right." She paused. "Okay, here's what happened. We met three weeks ago, fell madly in love and got engaged. My parents decided they had to meet the man who swept me off my feet, so they called this morning and told me they were driving up from Carmel to have dinner with us."

"Are your parents retired?"

"My mother thinks so, but my father has his own business and isn't ready for full-time retirement."

"What happened to the real fiancé?"

"What real fiancé?"

"I assume you told your family about a real engagement."

"No," Cassandra said. "I made it up."

She wasn't a compulsive liar, was she? "You told your family you were engaged when you weren't?"

She nodded.

"Why?"

She shrugged. "It seemed like the thing to do at the time. Sometimes, I'm, uh, impulsive." She smiled mischievously as if sharing a childhood secret.

He laughed. "I never would've guessed."

"I want to thank you, Troy." Her eyes shone with gratitude. "I could tell you were a nice guy. You have this wonderful aura."

Aura? He didn't know people who used words like that. Was she one of those New Agers? She did wear crystals, and she must be a little flaky to need a last-minute fiancé. Given he'd agreed to her crazy scheme, who was he to judge? Besides, too late to go back now. Tomorrow morning, he would be at the office working long hours. He could look back on tonight and laugh.

A smile lit up her beautiful face. "I don't know what I would have done if you hadn't said yes."

"Don't worry about it." Troy tried not to stare at her, but found it difficult. Especially with the way her dress was pulled tight across her chest, accentuating her full breasts.

Tonight looked better and better. He'd been working hard, trying to close the Micro-Psi deal and get offered a partnership with his firm. Life consisted of more than reading balance sheets and making deals. He was no different from any other red-blooded male. He needed a little rest and relaxation, too.

"No, it is a big deal." She squeezed his hand. "You're my McKnight in shining armor."

"At your service, milady. We McKnights aim to please." He wasn't sure if it was the full moon or her perfume, but he found her playful spirit contagious. When was the last time he'd had fun? Troy couldn't remember. "By the way, is there anything else I should know about tonight?"

"You should know a little about me." As she paused, she bit her lower lip. "Let's see. My favorite color is purple. I love flowers and hot fudge sundaes. I'm not a vegetarian because I love a good hamburger every now and then. Cooked medium, of course. I think people who won't eat veal, but eat chicken are hypocrites. I love reading books. I like one hundred percent cotton sheets and I sleep in the nude."

Stunned, Troy stared at her. She'd spoken so fast. Hot fudge sundaes and sleeping in the nude. His temperature rose a few degrees at the images filling his mind. He crossed his legs.

"What about you?"

He couldn't think straight. He needed to cool down. "Uh, I like ice cream."

"Chocolate's my favorite. What else?"

Troy stared into her eyes and found himself transfixed as if he were being hypnotized.

"Any sports?"

"I like football."

"What's your favorite color?"

Her eyes were the color of a cloudless, summer sky. "Blue."

She patted his hand. "Don't worry, we can make it up as we go along."

What was wrong with him? He felt out of sync. Almost dizzy. Maybe he needed something to eat.

The cab slowed as it approached the restaurant. Cassandra handed the driver a ten-dollar bill and slid out of the cab. "Are you ready?"

Why not? Troy cleared his throat. "Sure."

Cassandra brushed a lock of hair from his forehead

and straightened his tie. She took his hand in hers. "Don't forget, we're madly in love."

Her small hand fit snugly in his. Madly in love? Maybe they were just mad.

Without giving Troy time to change his mind, Cassandra bolted into the restaurant, pulling him with her. Hiding her nervousness was difficult. She wasn't a good actress, but if she pulled off tonight she should get an Oscar for her performance.

Cassandra searched for her family, but didn't see them standing at the carved Honduras mahogany bar. She did catch a glimpse of Troy's reflection in a mirror.

Luck was on her side tonight; he was perfect, exactly the fiancé she'd hoped to find. His navy Italian suit was top-of-the-line, silk cashmere if she guessed right, and custom-made. He even wore a Rolex.

With his high cheekbones and sculpted features, Troy looked like a Kennedy. All he needed was a different haircut. Still, she liked the way his almost-out-of-control curly brown hair added character to his all-American good looks.

Her picky parents would find little fault with Troy McKnight. They would give their seal of approval and stop interfering in her personal life. After tonight, their endless advice and matchmaking would stop. She'd be back on her own.

She smiled, pleased with herself. She'd found the perfect fiancé. Her sister, Emily, would be jealous, too. An added bonus. Cassandra didn't care what her brother-in-law, Eric, thought, as long as he didn't voice his opinion. She'd heard all she wanted to hear from Eric Wainwright. She'd be happier if she never had to see him again.

The hostess, an attractive woman with flaming red hair, led them to their table. Waiters hurried around with steaming plates of food and bottles of wine. The scent of basil and garlic drifted in the air. Cassandra hadn't eaten all day and was starving.

She didn't see an empty table in the crowded restaurant. The noise of spirited conversations rose from the tables, but it wasn't unpleasant. Not like at the Brewery where people went to be picked up. She hated that place, but she had found Troy there.

"Here's your party," the hostess said. "Enjoy your dinner, Ms. Daniels."

"Thank you." Cassandra took in the image of her family sitting at the table. They looked like a family from a magazine ad or a soap opera. She had tried fitting in, but realized that wasn't who she was. Maybe someday they would understand and accept the choices she'd made. Then again...

Her mother, Vanessa Daniels, wore a black St. John knit—her trademark. Every strand of her platinum hair was in place and her brilliant diamond earrings sparkled for all to admire. She was a stunning woman who looked like she was forty years old, not pushing sixty. Vanessa worked out every day to keep in shape. What would she do if she ever became a grandmother? Cassandra couldn't imagine her mother letting anyone call her grandma.

"I told you she would come, Emily," her mother crooned. "And look, her beau does exist."

Cassandra winced. She would show her parents she could find her own man. She didn't need their help, their interference.

"Sorry, we're late." Cassandra clutched Troy's warm, strong hand. She not only needed a fiancé tonight, but she also needed someone to give her emotional support. "Troy and I were making out in the back of the cab so I had the driver make an extra circle around the Civic Center."

Her mother blushed. "Cassandra, really."

"Don't worry, Vanessa." Her father, the venerable Dixon Daniels, downed his drink. His once-blond hair had turned gray and he could stand to lose about thirty pounds, but he was still handsome with sparkling, cornflower blue eyes and a cheerful smile. "At least this one looks normal. Unless there are hidden tattoos or pierced body parts under that suit."

Cassandra leaned over and kissed her father's tan cheek. The familiar scent of his aftershave filled her nostrils and brought back fond memories of her childhood. She might be the black sheep of the family, but she would always be daddy's little girl. "There's nothing hidden except a body to die for, Daddy."

"Cassandra, really." Her uptight sister, Emily, echoed their mother's favorite expression. "Don't you have any class?"

Class? Emily was mentioning *class?* "No, you got all of that when they divided the DNA."

Her fraternal twin, Emily was two minutes older, an inch taller and fifteen pounds lighter. She'd dyed her light brown hair jet black and wore it pulled back in a chignon. Her chic black dress shouted designer collection, but the sophisticated style didn't suit her. Two twins couldn't be more opposite. They had shared nothing except the same birth date, until Eric Wainwright.

Eric. Seeing him now, he looked pathetic. Sweat

beaded on his forehead, and he looked uncomfortable. A short, boring corporate hairstyle had replaced his luscious mane of blond hair. The hair—that's what had attracted Cassandra to him in the first place. It had given him a wildness and an edge that were missing now.

He'd reminded her of Brad Pitt in *Legends of the Fall*. She'd made the mistake of telling Eric that and he'd used the information to create a nineties version of the character Tristan. Who could blame her for falling in love with him?

But Cassandra had learned the nights riding on the back of his motorcycle and watching falling stars were only acts. Eric wanted a successful career. She had been his key, until he met Emily. In hindsight, things had worked out for the best. Cassandra only hoped he made her sister happy.

"Aren't you going to introduce us to your betrothed, sweetheart?" Dixon asked.

Her betrothed. Troy. With so much goodwill at the table, she'd almost forgotten the real reason for the family get-together—meeting her fiancé. As she cuddled against his firm, wide chest, his muscles tensed. "Troy, this is my family. Family, this is Troy McKnight, the man of my dreams."

After formal introductions, Cassandra and Troy sat. For several uncomfortable minutes, no one said anything. Cassandra ate a slice of bread before her stomach growled. She drank her entire glass of water, trying to wash away the dryness in her throat. The waiter came, took everyone's order and left. Still, no one spoke. She had to think of something to say and fast.

"I want to thank you for inviting us to dinner, Mr. and Mrs. Daniels." The genuine tone of Troy's voice surprised Cassandra. He raised his wineglass to acknowledge them.

"The pleasure is ours, Troy," her mother said, smiling. "And please call us Vanessa and Dixon. My husband's parents were Mr. and Mrs. Daniels."

Troy's smile reached all the way to the corners of his eyes. Cassandra had been more interested in his image, the whole package he presented, when she had picked him up. She hadn't realized how gorgeous he was.

"My mother says the same thing, Vanessa." Troy emphasized her first name. "Cassandra and I have been so wrapped up in each other that we've shut everyone out. I'm happy to meet you."

"We're happy, too." Dixon's assessing gaze never left Troy's eyes. "I must admit we were surprised, shocked really, when Cassandra told us about your engagement. After all, Emily and Eric had just returned from their honeymoon."

"How was your honeymoon?" Cassandra asked, trying to change the subject. Troy didn't need to know any of the details about her past with Eric.

"Wonderful," Eric answered. "It was everything we hoped it would be."

"Where did you go?" Troy asked, seemingly oblivious to the undercurrents at the table.

"The Mediterranean. We took a three-week cruise," Emily said before her husband could answer. "We made so many stops I lost count. It was fun, but tiring."

Eric cocked one eyebrow. "Have you made honeymoon plans?"

Cassandra suppressed the urge to toss a piece of bread at his oversize head. Instead she pasted on her most charming smile. ''Troy's in charge of the honeymoon.''

Without hesitation, Troy described his idea for their honeymoon. Two weeks of total relaxation on a tropical island with fine white sand, crystal blue water, a gentle sea breeze and no interruptions. She pictured Troy at the beach, bodysurfing in the waves, rubbing suntan lotion over her body, making…

Eric snickered. ''I can't imagine Cassandra sitting on a beach for two hours let alone two weeks.''

''We aren't planning to spend our time sitting,'' Troy answered with a wink, then bit into a slice of bread.

Cassandra's cheeks warmed. She could imagine falling for Mr. Troy McKnight.

Too bad he wasn't her type.

Not that she was interested in any type.

''Enough honeymoon talk.'' Dixon straightened in his chair. No doubt the thought of his daughters, married or not, having sex made him uncomfortable.

''Why don't we talk about the wedding?'' Vanessa suggested. ''Have you set a date?''

''No,'' Cassandra said. ''We aren't sure if we want a traditional wedding or not.''

''That doesn't surprise me,'' Emily muttered. ''I see you don't have a ring yet.''

''We're using my grandmother's engagement ring,'' Troy said to Cassandra's surprise. ''My parents are storing it, and I haven't had time to fly home and get it.''

''Your grandmother's ring.'' Vanessa clapped her hands together. ''A family heirloom. How wonderful.''

Troy smiled at Cassandra. Her mother's reaction seemed to please him.

Eric glanced at the rock on Emily's ring finger. "That works out well. Troy has a ring to use and Cassandra has a dress to wear."

Cassandra balled her hands into fists. She noticed the silent exchange between her sister and Eric. Even Emily looked surprised by his statement.

"She can't wear that dress, Eric," Emily said with uncharacteristic understanding. "She bought it for... you."

"But the dress has never been worn," Eric explained. "It would be a waste to let the gown hang in the closet forever."

Cassandra tensed. Troy placed his arm around her shoulder and pulled her close. His warm breath teased her neck.

"Are you okay?" he whispered.

She nodded. At least someone cared, or pretended to care, about her feelings. "I sold the dress."

"This time—" Vanessa picked up her glass of Chardonnay "—I want to go shopping with you."

"Of course, Mother." That day would never happen.

"There's plenty of time to talk about the wedding," Dixon said. "All I know is my little girl looks happy and that makes me happy."

"My job is to make her happy." Troy caressed her cheek with his fingertips.

A tingle ran down Cassandra's spine. "And you do an excellent job." *Did he ever.* She would have to be careful.

"So what is your real job, Troy?" Emily asked.

*The interrogation begins.* Leave it to her sister to

get down to the bottom line—income potential. This should be interesting. Cassandra assumed Troy was an attorney. He had that overpaid lawyer look about him. "Go ahead, honey. Tell them what you do."

Troy cleared his throat. "Venture capital."

Oh, no. Not V.C. This couldn't be happening. Cassandra clenched her teeth to keep her mouth from gaping open.

Dixon beamed. He was one of the kings of venture capitalists, financiers who invest in start-up companies in hopes of making huge profits. "I thought you looked familiar, Troy. Who do you work for, Sand Hill? No, it's Scorpio Partners. I remember now. You handled the MagicSoft deal."

Troy nodded.

"Very impressive," Dixon said. He wasn't a man who gave praise often. "Why didn't you tell me your fiancé was in the business, honey?"

Cassandra searched her mind for an answer. Troy had caught her off guard. He looked liked an attorney; he was supposed to be an attorney.

How could she have been so stupid? Why hadn't she asked what he did? Daniels Venture Group was one of the most respected and well-known firms in Silicon Valley. Every up and coming V.C. would kill to learn from the master, Dixon Daniels. Marrying the boss's daughter was an easy way in. Just ask Eric Wainwright. "Well, Dad—"

"We wanted to tell you in person," Troy said. "I didn't want you to think I was marrying your daughter for the wrong reasons."

Dixon glanced at Eric, then back at Troy. "Does this mean you have no interest in joining my group?"

Cassandra stared at Troy, unsure if she wanted to

hear his answer. Eric had lied when she had asked him the same question. She crumpled the linen napkin on her lap.

"I wouldn't say I have no interest, but my first concern is Cassie."

Cassie? She hadn't been called Cassie since she had graduated from high school and *demanded* to be called Cassandra.

Troy continued. "Getting married is stressful. A new job would only add to the pressure. I want to be the best fiancé and husband I can, so I don't see making any changes in the near future."

Cassandra smiled, feeling a rush of emotion build up. She'd always hoped to find a man who would say those words, to put her needs ahead of his own. Troy answered the question well; he even sounded sincere. Maybe not all men were like Eric. Perhaps some were like Troy.

After all, he was the perfect fiancé, at least for tonight. And Troy would make a great husband. A great husband for someone else, she thought with a twinge of regret. She wasn't in the market for a husband.

"Cassandra, you've found such a nice man. He's perfect." Vanessa dabbed her eyes with a handkerchief. "It took me hours to do my makeup. I can't believe I'm going to ruin it."

"You don't need makeup to look beautiful, Vanessa," Dixon said.

She sniffled. "I hope you will be very happy together."

"Vanessa, you read my mind." Dixon raised his glass. "A toast…to Troy and Cassie. May the two of you find a lifetime of happiness together."

Oh, no, her father called her Cassie. She had spent

her freshman year of college convincing her family to call her by her full name. Of course, she'd later realized she was more of a Cassie than a Cassandra, but by then the trench had been dug too deep and she had to continue holding her ground. "Daddy?"

"Yes, Cassie?"

The joy in his eyes made her hesitate. For the first time in years, she had made him happy. Her mother looked equally pleased. Cassandra couldn't spoil it, not yet anyway. She swallowed the lump in her throat. "Thank you."

"So, Cassie," Emily said with a saccharine sweet tone. "Have you heard we've been house hunting? Unfortunately the market is tight, especially in Palo Alto."

"I bet."

"Are you still living in that...unique little apartment on Twenty-fourth Street?"

No. Thanks to her and Eric. They were the reason Cassandra had moved. As her temper flared, she reached for her glass of Cabernet. She sipped slowly, enjoying the robust taste of the full-bodied wine until she reined in her emotions. "No, I live a couple of blocks away."

"You should buy a place. Renting makes no sense."

"It's like flushing your money down the toilet." Cassandra smiled, ending her sister's lecture.

The rest of the evening went remarkably well. Melt-in-your-mouth desserts followed the savory dinner. Cassandra managed to be civil to Emily and Eric, who returned the politeness. Troy charmed his way further into her parents' heart. Everything had gone according to plan except for her father continuing to call her Cassie, but she could fix that later.

As she followed her parents outside, she couldn't believe how easily things had worked out. Cassandra kissed her mother's cheek. "It was wonderful seeing you."

"I enjoyed it, dear. I like your young man," Vanessa whispered.

"Thanks, Mom." Cassandra hugged her father. "Thanks for the delicious dinner, Daddy."

"Glad you could come." Dixon released her. He extended his arm to Troy. "And I'm happy we got to spend time with you."

Troy shook his hand. "Thanks for dinner, sir."

"I wish we had more time to get to know one another," Dixon said, a twinge of regret in his voice.

"Daddy, it's getting late." Emily tapped her foot on the sidewalk. "You and mother have a long drive ahead of you."

"We're staying in the city, so don't worry about us," Dixon said. "I have an idea. Are you a golfer, Troy?"

"Yes, but I'm a hacker."

"Me, too." Dixon's tone made Cassandra bite back a chuckle. Her father, who played at least three days a week, had a four handicap. He was far from a hacker. "Why don't you and Cassie spend the weekend with us in Carmel? You and I can golf, and the women can discuss wedding plans. Short notice, I realize."

"Uh." Troy ran his hand through his hair. "What do you think, honey?"

"Well, I—"

"It's settled," Dixon said before Cassandra could

say no. He placed something in Troy's hand and whispered in his ear.

"Daddy…"

Dixon kissed her cheek. "We'll see you Friday night, kids."

With that, her parents walked around the corner. Emily and Eric followed them. Cassandra stared at the deserted sidewalk, unable to believe what had happened. Her shoulders slumped.

"It was going so well. Too well, of course. I can't believe I didn't see this coming. I wanted them to like you, but this is too much." Turning to face Troy, she frowned. "How are we going to get out of this?"

With a bewildered look, he stared at the contents in his hand. "I don't know."

"What did my father give you?"

Troy showed her two twenty-dollar bills. "You won't believe what he said it was for."

# 2

———◆———

Cassandra stared at the money in Troy's hand. "I can't believe my father gave you gas money."

"Me, either," Troy said with an incredulous look on his face. "I'm thirty years old. No one's ever given me gas money. Not even my own father."

"It's not a big deal. He's done it all my life. I don't bother arguing with him anymore. It's futile."

"I don't need your father's money." Troy's eyebrows furrowed. Her explanation didn't mollify him in the least. "I might not have my own company or fund, but I have a good job."

"This isn't about you," Cassandra explained, wondering if Troy took everything so seriously. He needed to lighten up a bit. "He did it for me. He's trying to take care of his little girl."

"But I feel…offended," Troy said. "I can take care of you myself."

"I know that and so does my father." Cassandra wished she'd brought a jacket with her. As usual, San Francisco weather had dropped to a biting cold. Goose bumps covered her skin and she crossed her arms. "Be happy my father likes you."

Troy removed his suit jacket and placed it around her shoulders. "He does?"

"Of course, much to my brother-in-law's chagrin." Cassandra laughed. "Did you see the way Eric glared at you? The look on his face was priceless. I'm sure he thinks you're trying to grab a share of his gravy train."

Troy tightened his lips into a narrow line. "You think this is funny, Cassie?"

"It's Cassandra and yes, I do." The tone of his voice annoyed her. "Relax, Troy. It's forty dollars. My father did not mean to offend you, so stop feeling insulted. Consider it payment for services rendered. Use it for your cab fare home. I'll come up with some excuse why we can't make it this weekend. This is my problem, not yours."

"I disagree." He shoved the forty dollars into her hand. "This goes beyond gas money, Cassie. It's as much my problem as yours."

"Why is that?"

"Your father is Dixon Daniels." Troy said her father's name with an almost reverent tone. "It doesn't matter whether I want to work for him or not, but I have my reputation and career to consider. Dixon is an influential man in the V.C. circle. I doubt he'd be spiteful on purpose, but as you pointed out you are his daughter."

How dare he, a total stranger, criticize her father. She clenched her hands into fists. "My father would not sabotage your career. He is an honorable man."

"An honorable man who adores you, Cassie," Troy said softly. "I was tempted to walk out when I saw him, but I couldn't leave you there alone."

At least she'd picked an honorable fiancé. "Thanks for staying." She bit her lower lip, struggling to put the situation into perspective.

"Don't you see, Cassie? I can't blow you off like a one-night stand and risk offending your father. I'm not a partner in a V.C. Fund. I'm an associate, working my way up the proverbial ladder. If he wanted, Dixon could become a big obstacle to my getting ahead."

"What are you suggesting we do?" Cassandra asked, not sure if she wanted to hear his idea. She wasn't happy being stuck with his honorable intentions now.

He glanced at the sidewalk and muttered something. She couldn't have heard him correctly. "What did you say?"

"I said we could be engaged for a little while longer."

"Are you crazy?" She yelled so loudly, passengers in a passing car stopped to ask if she was all right.

"Until tonight, I would have said no," Troy said with a half smile. "Are you seeing anyone?"

"What does that have to do—"

"Answer the question, Cassie."

"No."

"Neither am I," Troy said. "So we don't have to worry about other people. I don't see why it wouldn't work."

*It's crazy, that's why.* The situation was getting out of control. Not that this mess wasn't her fault. She took full responsibility for the fiasco they faced, but that didn't mean she had to let it continue. No, she had to put a stop to it. "That's what I said about tonight and look where we are now."

Troy didn't listen. Instead he buttoned the front of his jacket around her. "Once your parents see how different we are, they'll understand when we break up.

We can say goodbye and tell your parents it's too painful to remain friends.''

Although Cassandra didn't think her father could hurt Troy's career, she understood his concern. She had dragged him into this mess. Was she willing to take a chance with Troy's job hanging in the balance?

"How often do you see your parents?" he asked.

*Never.* "Not much."

"So no one will know whether we are still together or not. All we have to do is get through the weekend."

*The weekend.*

As much as she might want to make a clean break, Cassandra couldn't leave Troy in the lurch. He seemed like a nice enough guy. A little uptight, but he'd gone along with her charade. It wasn't fair to leave him with a noose around his neck and her father holding the rope. "How long will we keep up the masquerade?"

"Long enough so I don't look like a jerk." His smile lightened the seriousness of their situation. "What do you think? Will you be my fiancée for the weekend or not?"

She had wanted a fiancé for the night, not any longer. She enjoyed her life the way it was—uncomplicated. "Okay, but on one condition."

"Name it."

"We don't get married," she said half joking, half serious. "I mean, let's not get carried away with this, uh, thing. I've already had one fiancé who was more interested in marrying my father than me."

"That's an easy one." Troy laughed. "I don't want to marry Dixon."

She exhaled slowly. "That's not what I meant."

"I know." Troy smiled. "I promise not to get carried away with this 'thing.'"

"Thank you."

"Besides, Cassie," he said, almost laughing again. "Could you imagine us married?"

After his night of adventure, Troy dreamed of chocolate ice cream, hot fudge, whipped cream and Cassie. He overslept and raced to catch the Marina Express, bus number 30X. He arrived at his office an hour late. His boss, Mick, met him at the door.

"Late night, Troy?"

"I—"

"Don't worry about it," Mick said with a Cheshire-cat smile. "Why don't you come into my office?"

What had he done? Troy couldn't imagine being called into Mick's office because he was an hour late. Besides, Mick had a smile on his face. Something was up, but what?

As Troy followed his boss, he noticed the sympathetic smile of a young researcher. Another one snickered. Mick was a fair man who demanded and rewarded hard work. He had a temper, though, and rarely took employees into his office unless it was to chastise them. He believed in airing grievances in private, away from the watchful eyes and ears of the office staff. As Troy walked past Mick's secretary, she gave him the thumbs-up sign. Must not be too bad with Della so relaxed.

Inside the office, Troy glanced around. A picture of Mick's gorgeous wife and another picture of his midnight blue BMW hung on the wall. At thirty-seven, Mick had it all. And Troy wanted it—his own fund, a chrome-and-glass decorated corner office, a view of the Golden Gate Bridge, a luxurious car and a wife who looked like a *Sports Illustrated* swimsuit model. If he stuck to his plan, he'd have it all, too.

"Have a seat."

Troy sat on a black leather chair.

Mick pushed aside a pile of files and a stack of *Wall Street Journal*s. He leaned against the edge of his desk. "Anything new?"

Start on a good note. Mick believed in bragging if one could back it up. "I think we're going to close on the Micro-Psi deal by Friday."

"Excellent." Mick rolled his shoulders as though he were trying to relax his muscles. "Anything else?"

"I—"

"I got an interesting phone call this morning," Mick interrupted. "From Dixon Daniels."

*Damn.*

"He wanted to talk about you," Mick said nonchalantly as if it didn't matter.

*Dammit.*

"He asked all sorts of interesting questions." Mick's gaze bored into him. A vein on the side of his neck throbbed. The cutthroat negotiator, as competitors often called him, broke through Mick's seemingly laid-back manner.

*Oh hell.*

"Man-to-man, Troy," Mick said in a serious tone with one black eyebrow cocked. "What's going on?"

*I met a woman last night and agreed to be her fiancé not knowing her father was Dixon Daniels.* Mick wouldn't understand. Over the last three years, Troy had learned one thing about his boss—outside of making investments, Mick never took risks. "Nothing."

Mick took a deep breath, then exhaled slowly. "I know people are always looking for better opportunities, but I thought you were happy here."

"I—"

"You told me you were ready for more money, additional responsibilities, but I've been slow in responding. What if I increased your annual bonus by twenty percent?"

*Twenty percent.* He could pay for a new roof on his parents' house; he could pay off some of his student loans. Troy held back a smile. "It's a start."

"Daniels is a fine man, but we have an excellent group here. You're a key player in our team." Mick cracked his knuckles. "We're starting a new fund early next year. I mentioned a possible partnership when I hired you. Is that something you'd be interested in?"

*Partnership. Wow.* He'd sell his soul for a partnership in the new fund. It's what he'd been working for these past three years. "I'd be interested."

"I need to talk to the other partners, of course. This is an involved process."

"Of course." Troy wished he could high-five his boss, but maintained his calm. His mind reeled with the possibility of being made a partner, but one nagging thought kept intruding into his excitement. "I need to ask you one thing, Mick."

"Ask away."

"Are you offering me all of this because Dixon Daniels called or because I deserve it?"

"Excellent question." Mick grinned. "What do you think?"

Over the last three years, Troy had made solid deals and big profits for Mick. "Because I deserve it."

"You deserve it, Troy," Mick said with conviction. "Let's say Dixon gave me the kick in the ass I needed to do something about it."

"Thanks, Mick."

He winked and stood. "You stay with me and I'll make it worth your while."

*Yes.* Troy rose, unable to believe he was on-track with his plan. This would put him a year ahead of schedule for a partnership. "I'll think about it."

Mick patted Troy's shoulder. "It's going to be difficult to say no to Dixon, he's a tough one."

"I can handle it." At this moment, Troy could handle anything. He felt as if he could soar out of the window on the forty-seventh floor and fly. His dreams were finally coming true.

"I'm sure you can." Mick opened the door to his office. "Maybe you can get Dixon interested in one of our deals. Talk about a coup. None of our partners have been able to do that."

And Troy doubted he'd be able to, either. Oh, well, might as well play it for all it's worth. "You never know."

"I like your attitude." Mick's smile widened. "Have an excellent day."

"I will."

Troy walked to his desk and sat on his canvas-covered chair. A well-deserved increase in his yearly bonus and a partnership were within his reach. He thought about his master plan, the one he'd followed since deciding to go to business school and make something out of himself. He was achieving all he'd planned, but...

He'd taken the job with Mick and never considered changing companies. Troy figured hard work and loyalty would earn him high marks and even greater rewards. After the close of the MagicSoft deal, he thought he would be offered a partnership, but he wasn't.

Until today. Thanks to catalyst Dixon Daniels. Troy didn't feel comfortable with the help. He was willing to do what it took to get what he wanted, but...

How long would it have taken Mick to act without the call from Dixon? Maybe Troy needed to reexamine his plan. If he'd stuck to his plan and acted like Mick, Troy would have never agreed to pose as Cassie's fiancé.

Cassie. The not-his-type charmer.

He preferred women with classic style—tailored clothes, subdued jewelry and impeccable makeup. Cassandra Daniels had created her own style and there was nothing classic about it.

Still, he had to smile. For a perfect stranger, she'd had a significant impact on his life. She was also giving him something else—a weekend with Dixon Daniels. How many V.C. associates got the opportunity to spend time with a legend?

Troy wanted to call her, to thank her. They were supposed to talk tomorrow to make plans for Friday's drive to Carmel, but today was a special day. Surely that justified the call. It wasn't as if he was asking her out. He merely wanted to talk to her. Troy pulled out her telephone number from his wallet and dialed.

On the fourth ring, she answered.

"Hello?" Her voice sounded husky.

"Hi, it's Troy."

"Troy, who?"

For an airhead, he remembered, she was well connected. He released an exasperated sigh. "Troy McKnight, your fiancé."

"Oh, that Troy," she said. "I'm sorry. I'm still in bed."

In bed? Their conversation in the cab came rushing back. Troy imagined her naked body between one hundred percent cotton sheets. The feel of her soft skin, the scent of her... What was he thinking? Cassie was a Roman candle about to burn his hand. "I'm sorry I called so early."

"No problem."

Not for her, at least.

"Are you okay?" she asked, her sweet voice full of concern.

"Yes, but Cassie?"

"It's Cassandra, go on."

She would always be Cassie to him. "Dixon called my boss this morning."

"Why?" She sounded alarmed. "What did he want?"

"Nothing important. He asked my boss, Mick, some questions."

He could picture her biting her lower lip. "What questions?"

"Mick didn't say, but he increased my annual bonus and talked about making me a partner."

"I'm sure my father had nothing to do with it. I'm sure you're a hard worker and deserve it."

He laughed at the way she tried to justify his good fortune. "I do deserve it, but your father made Mick realize I have other options. He made me realize that, too. I have you to thank. Our so-called engagement is actually helping me." And could help him further. Who knew what pearls of wisdom he could pick up from Dixon Daniels over the course of a weekend? This was looking better and better.

"You're not angry?"

Troy picked up a pen. "No."

"I thought after the gas money thing—"

"This is different." He twirled the pen with his fingers. "Maybe I should be angry, but actually I'm happy."

"You deserve to be happy, Troy," she said. "You'll have to go out and celebrate."

Celebrate? If he went out with the guys, he'd only end up with a hangover the next morning. And what guys? Most were married with babies now. But he did deserve a celebration. Maybe Cassie would want to go. "Would you like to join me?"

"When?"

*Why is she asking?* It wasn't like a date or anything. "Tonight?"

Silence.

Why the long pause? Static filled his receiver. He twirled the pen round and round. A phone rang somewhere else in the office. "Do you have other plans tonight?"

"No."

If he didn't give her a good reason for meeting him, she would say no. "Cassie, we are going to be spending the weekend together pretending to be engaged. We need to learn more about each other so we don't make any mistakes. I want this weekend to go well, don't you?"

*See, no date. A research meeting.* Troy smiled at the reasoning. He almost believed it himself, but he couldn't erase the image of Cassie between the sheets.

"Yes," she said finally. "I'm free after eight."

"Where do you live?" Troy asked, curious about what would keep her busy until eight o'clock.

"Uh, Noe Valley."

"Do you want me to come there?"

"Why don't we meet by your place since you're the one sacrificing a weekend to go to my parents' house?"

"Sounds fair." He ignored a twinge of disappointment. He wanted to see where Cassie lived; he wanted to learn more about her. "Say nine o'clock, at the coffeehouse on the corner of Chestnut and Avila."

"You live in the Marina?"

"Yes."

"Figures."

"What's that supposed to mean, Cassie?"

"Nothing," she replied. "I'll see you tonight."

"I'm looking forward to it." As Troy hung up the phone, he realized a scary thought—he was looking forward to seeing Cassie.


Cassandra stepped off the bus at the corner of Fillmore and Chestnut. Walking toward the coffeehouse, she wove her way through the couples and groups of young professionals crowding the sidewalks on their way to one of the many restaurants, bars and shops on Chestnut Street.

The Marina District. Cassandra fought the rush of memories. She'd tried to erase everything about her old life—the one her family had approved of, the stressful life that had nearly given her an ulcer. Maybe she'd done too good a job. She hadn't been here in a long time. In a strange way it felt good to be back, but the street wasn't the same.

A Pottery Barn had replaced the all-night market.

When she had lived here, she used to stop in on her way home from work. No matter what the time, the store always had what she wanted. A bar had replaced the toy store. She counted three juice bars and a new ice-cream place. Chestnut Street had changed and become more upscale than before. She didn't know if the changes were for the better, but she hoped the displaced merchants had found better opportunities elsewhere.

Cassandra stopped on the corner across from the coffeehouse. Two women wearing in-line skates sat outside at a small, round table. The place looked crowded.

What was she doing here? All day, Cassandra had thought about meeting Troy. As she'd shelved books in the travel section of her bookstore, she'd daydreamed about a tropical island with hourglass fine sand and turquoise water. Troy had played a starring role. She couldn't understand why. He seemed down-to-earth, but that's what she'd thought about Eric. Until Emily.

Thinking about Troy in any way other than casual acquaintance made zero sense. Look at the situation. Troy was pretending to be her fiancé. Did that make him dishonest? Like Eric? And what did that say about her since it was her idea?

Not that it mattered. Troy was everything she wasn't—ambitious, cautious, rigid.

Still, he intrigued her, and men rarely intrigued her. She didn't want them to. It wasn't worth the risk.

Something about Troy, though. Cassandra couldn't put her finger on it—maybe his polite manners, maybe the twinkle of mischief in his eyes. Whatever it was, she wanted to learn more about her so-called fiancé. And that bothered her, more than she wanted to admit.

Cassandra glanced at her watch. Quarter after nine. Only a little late. Squaring her shoulders, she made her way into the jam-packed coffee house. Alternative rock music blared from the overhead speakers. Customers crammed into the place. Every table was taken with people trying to talk over the music and other conversations. Two men played backgammon at a small square table; a man and a woman played Scrabble at another. She spotted Troy, reading the *Wall Street Journal* at a table in the back.

"Hi," she said. "Sorry I'm late."

As he folded his paper, he stood. "Let me guess, you're always late."

His smile sent her stomach into cartwheels. "Yes, and I bet you're always early."

"Usually."

His punctuality didn't surprise her. And she would bet he even arrived on his expected due date. Troy McKnight was the kind of man to have scheduled his own birth. Good thing they weren't engaged. She couldn't handle living like that.

Standing on her tiptoes, she kissed his cheek. "For practice, of course."

"Of course."

She pulled a green lollipop out of her purse and handed it to him. "Congratulations."

"Thanks." He laughed at the dollar sign on the candy. "You didn't have to get me anything."

"No," she said. "But I wanted to."

Reaching across the table, he pulled out a chair for her. "Have a seat."

She tossed her sweater over the back and sat. "What would you like to drink?"

"It's my treat, Cassie."

"I..." Tonight was his night so she would allow him to pay and let the name slide. "Since you're on your way to megabucks, I'll have a latte."

"I'll be right back."

As she sat at the table, Troy placed his order at the counter. She couldn't help but notice the assessing and approving glances of other women. She couldn't blame them. He looked so relaxed and casual in a pair of khakis and a navy polo shirt. Not at all like the businessman she'd found last night. Thank goodness he'd ditched the silk tie and button-down shirt. Only his ruffled hair looked the same.

He placed two steaming cups on the table. "Here you go."

"Thanks." She picked up the warm cup. "To your prosperous future."

Troy clicked his cup against hers. "This is a great way to end an equally great day."

As she stared at his long, thick eyelashes, she almost drifted back into one of her daydreams of the clothing-optional tropical island. Cassandra hadn't noticed his lush lashes last night. She wet her dry lips.

Enough. Stop admiring him. She couldn't stand any more complications, and Troy McKnight would be a huge one. Any man would be.

Cassandra sipped her latte. Too bad the hot liquid only added to the heat building within her.

"I've been thinking about this weekend." Troy set his cup on the table. "I need it to go well, especially after talking to Mick today."

"We wouldn't want to ruin your good fortune."

"Especially since the partnership is not a sure thing," Troy said. "You know, we're going to have to act like an engaged couple. But it'll only be for forty-eight hours."

Forty-eight hours didn't sound too long. "I can handle it."

"Do the terms honey or sweetheart offend you?"

Not bad, a politically correct fiancé. "I can live with them, what about you, darling?"

His eyes widened and he sat straighter in his chair.

She laughed. "You're not the only one who gets to use terms of endearment, oh, love of my life. I hope you can live with the kissing and hugging and touching and—"

"I get the picture." He took another sip of his coffee. "How do you want to start?"

Time to ruffle a few of those stiff feathers of his. She caressed the top of his hand. "Do you mean with the kissing and touch—"

"No, with getting to know each other."

"I ask a question, then you ask one." She enjoyed the way she had him squirming in his seat. This was turning out to be more fun than she thought it would be.

"Sounds democratic," he said.

"You can start, since it's your celebration."

"How old are you?" Troy asked.

"Twenty-eight," she said. "How old are you?"

"Thirty."

"It's your turn," she said when he didn't ask his question.

Troy started, then checked himself.

"Just ask. I won't be offended."

He paused. "I don't mean to pry."

"What do you want to know?"

"Are you in love with Eric?"

"No," she said without hesitation. That was an easy one.

"*No,* that's it?"

"You already asked your question, it's my turn," she said, not wanting to explore her relationship with Eric Wainwright any further. She hoped she didn't sound too defensive. Nervous, she tapped her foot.

"Can I continue, please?" Troy asked.

So much for fun. She saw the compassion in his eyes. What could it hurt? After all they were supposed to be engaged. Well, sort of engaged. "Go ahead."

"If you're not in love with him, why did you need a fiancé last night?"

Unrequited love. So that's what Troy thought. Politically correct and a romantic. Not a bad combination. He didn't want to hurt her. He wanted to know for some reason. She stopped tapping her foot. "I didn't need a fiancé because of Eric."

Troy's eyes narrowed. "Then who?"

"It's not important. Don't you love the smell of freshly brewed coffee?" Cassandra asked, trying to change the subject.

Troy didn't bite. "Who? Your sister?"

"My parents." She swirled the contents of her cup. "They…it's a long story."

"I'm not going anywhere." Troy sipped his coffee.

"Eric and I broke up over a year ago," she explained, hoping Troy didn't ask why. Both Emily and Eric had betrayed her, but it wasn't public knowledge. "After the wedding was canceled, I wasn't interested in dating."

"Or haven't been interested in dating since then?"

How could Cassandra trust anyone when she didn't trust her own sister? But it was more than that. She'd been hurt and she didn't want it to happen again. Cassandra shrugged. "What's the old adage, once bitten, twice shy?"

Troy said nothing, but motioned for her to continue.

"About six months ago, my parents invited me and a date to dinner. I wasn't seeing anyone, so I asked a friend." She smiled. "Some of my friends are a bit unconventional."

"Pierced body parts?"

She nodded. "Rascal is very nice. He'd give you the shirt off his tattooed back if you asked."

Troy laughed. "I assume your parents weren't thrilled meeting Rascal."

"You assume correctly. A couple of weeks after the infamous dinner I bumped into my parents near Union Square. I was with another friend who happens to be a biker." She laughed, remembering the horrified look on her mother's face. "My mother couldn't take it. Otto was wearing a spiked collar and black leather."

"So your parents were concerned about the men you were dating?"

"Concerned is putting it mildly, and I wasn't even dating them," she said. Now it seemed almost funny. At the time she'd been humiliated by the way her phone had rung off the hook. Humiliating enough that she invented a mythical fiancé. "All of a sudden I'm getting phone calls from men, sons and grandsons of my parents' friends, asking me out on dates. My mother suggests I go into therapy or join a support group. My father tells me to join a health club or a singles club so I can meet suitable suitors. It drove me crazy."

"You're lucky they care so much."

"I know they love me, but I couldn't stand their interference. I figured a make-believe fiancé would be the easy way out. They could stop worrying and I could have my life back."

"Only you don't have your life back, do you?" he asked, sounding almost regretful.

His gentle voice, the tenderness in his eyes tugged at Cassandra's heart. She wondered how many hearts Troy McKnight had broken. Several, if her intuition were on track. She wouldn't want to join the list; she couldn't afford to join the list. "Not yet, but I will soon, won't I?"

# 3

She drove him nuts.

What had Troy been thinking? Dealing with the wrath of Dixon Daniels would be easier than fighting his own raging hormones. After being crammed in the cab of his small pickup with Cassie for the past two and a half hours, Troy was reaching his breaking point. At least his zipper was.

He gripped the steering wheel until his knuckles turned white. He enjoyed talking with her, but every time she turned her head, he caught a whiff of perfume, shampoo, soap—her. She smelled fresh, a bit like citrus. He felt as if he had completed a triathalon and desperately needed a cool drink. Cassie was a glass of lemonade on a hot summer day. Troy wanted to taste her, to quench his thirst.

He was in over his head.

For the last three days, he had thought about her at the most inopportune times—doodling her name during a MagicSoft board meeting and suggesting the name Cass Ale for a new beer during a meeting with a brewery.

Cassie spelled danger.

Troy even found her clothes a turn-on. And that surprised him. Nothing she wore could be considered "fitted" or "tailored." Baggy, perhaps. Today, her oversize yellow sweater, calf-length gauze skirt and brown boots covered everything except her neck and head, but she looked sexier than the women wearing skimpy bikinis on "Baywatch." It was a miracle he'd made it to Carmel without driving off the road. Luckily Cassie seemed not to notice. She questioned him about his background and seemed more interested in hearing about growing up in Missouri and his big family, than anything else.

"Turn right," she said, as they drove along a tree-lined street with large, well-kept houses on either side. "Stop on the driveway. The gate should open automatically."

Troy stopped in front of a pair of closed wrought-iron gates. Suddenly they opened as if on cue.

"Keep following the driveway."

What kind of house needed a gated entrance? As he drove, he found out. In the distance, a two-story house stood out against the horizon. Like a Mediterranean Villa, the white stucco house had archways, terraces and balconies. Dixon Daniels had made a lot of money, especially in the early days of computers and telecommunications, but Troy hadn't expected a house, an estate, this sprawling.

*Someday. Someday, I'm going to live in a place like this. First step, becoming a partner.*

As he turned off the ignition, Dixon walked out to greet them. This had better work, Troy thought, feeling as though his career hung by a thin, unraveling string.

Cassie slid out of the front seat. She greeted her father with a hug. "Hi, Dad."

"Good to see you, sweetheart." Dixon studied Troy's truck. "Nice truck. Practical, too."

Troy cleared his throat. He'd tried to rent a better car, but couldn't find what he was looking for. Thank goodness he'd washed the truck before coming. "It gets me around."

"Does it have four-wheel drive?"

"Yes."

"Good in snow, I'll bet." Dixon smiled. "We have a cabin in Tahoe. Do you ski?"

Cabin? Troy bet it was more like a lodge. "I love to ski."

"How was the drive?"

*Sixty-five all the way, sir. Not.* "Fine."

"Did you take Highway 1?"

"Yes."

"It's a beautiful drive." Dixon smiled as Troy nodded in agreement. "Did you hit much traffic?"

"A little in Half Moon Bay." Troy grabbed the bags and his golf clubs from the back of the pickup. Surprisingly Cassie's flowered print bag was smaller and lighter than his.

Dixon took her bag from Troy's hand. "Vanessa's fixing a snack. I hope you're hungry, son."

Son? Dixon said the word as if he meant it. Troy swallowed the sudden lump of guilt lodged in his throat. Respected and liked in the industry, Dixon made killer deals and never showed any weaknesses. But Troy saw one now. Dixon Daniels was a powerful and intelligent businessman, but he had an Achilles' heel—his daughters. "I'm starved."

Cassie took her father's hand. "We didn't want to arrive too late so we didn't stop for dinner."

"You should always eat, Cassie," Dixon said like

a typical father. "Troy, make sure she eats three meals a day. If she doesn't, she gets cranky."

"Daddy," Cassie said, sounding horrified. She pursed her lips. "I'm never cranky. Emily's the one who needs to eat, not me."

With his forehead wrinkled, Dixon looked deep in thought. "It is your sister," he said finally. "I'm sorry, sweetheart. Troy, forget what I said."

As Cassie entered the house, Dixon grabbed his shoulder, holding him back. "Cassie gets cranky, too," he whispered. "Make sure she eats."

Troy chuckled. "I will."

He stepped inside wondering if he'd stepped into a layout for *Architectural Digest.* Terra-cotta tiles covered the entryway. Original artwork, illuminated by recessed lights, hung on the textured walls.

"Leave your bags in the entryway. We'll take them upstairs later," Dixon said. "Let's go into the living room."

Cassie took Troy's hand and led him into the large living room filled with elegant furniture. He'd grown up with five brothers and sisters in a four-bedroom farmhouse in the middle of nowhere. The sculpture in the corner of the room probably cost more than refurnishing his parents' house after a flood destroyed everything. The painting over the fireplace would pay off the mortgage on the farm.

Cassie stopped in front of an elaborate flower arrangement. She broke a lily from its stem and tucked it behind her ear.

Dixon motioned him to sit. "Have a seat, Troy."

The white couch looked too clean to sit on, but Cassie pulled him down next to her. As she and Dixon chatted, Troy took in the room. He wasn't much into interior decorating, but he recognized quality. He'd visited mansions in Pacific Heights and estates in Hillsborough. He'd been impressed by more than a couple of places, but this house overwhelmed him.

Cassie elbowed him. "Honey, do you want a drink?"

"Sure, thanks."

"What would you like, sweetheart, a beer?" Cassie asked.

As Troy nodded, Dixon spoke up. "I'll have one, too."

"But, Daddy, you always drink—"

"I want a beer," Dixon said with authority, ending further discussion.

Cassie kissed Troy's cheek. "I'll be right back, sugar."

"Don't forget to see if your mother needs any help," Dixon added as she left the room. "You're going to have your hands full with her, Troy."

He already did. "I can handle her."

"Vanessa spoiled both of the girls."

From what Troy had seen when picking Cassie up, she seemed remarkably unspoiled. She lived in a Victorian flat with peeling paint and squeaky steps. Her wardrobe consisted of casual and eclectic clothes. No designer labels that he could tell.

"I suppose I had a hand in spoiling them, too. It's difficult not to when we have all of this." Dixon glanced around the room until his gaze rested on a picture of his two daughters. The portrait showed a younger Emily and Cassie. Both wore sweaters and strands of pearl. Cassie looked so…normal.

"When was the portrait done?" Troy asked.

"After they graduated from college."

"Cassie looks so—"

"Different," Dixon said.

"Yes."

"She was, but... Let's just say, Cassie got my stubborn streak. Once she makes a decision, there's no turning back. And she'll go to the extreme to prove her point."

"She's strong-willed," Troy said. "I respect that."

"Good." Dixon smiled. "But remember, she'll always assume she's right. Compromise isn't one of her strong points. Don't let her get away with too much, Troy."

He didn't understand what Dixon was trying to say, but since Troy wasn't going to marry her it didn't matter. "Cassie and I will do fine."

"It makes me happy to hear that." Dixon smiled. "So, tell me. How is Mick treating you at the office? Has he offered you a partnership yet?"

Her mother was cooking and her father wanted a beer? Who were these strangers? Aliens, perhaps. Where were her real parents?

Cassandra entered the kitchen. A pan of brownies sat on the stove. Her mother stood at the granite counter, working on a tray of vegetables.

She blinked, wondering if the image would disappear. "Can I help, Mom?"

Vanessa turned and smiled. Usually the definition of refinement and elegance, she wore a pale pink apron over her black knit pants and white knit blouse. "I didn't hear you come in. I told your father to let me know when you arrived."

"He sent me in for beers. I think he wants to talk to Troy alone."

"I'm sure of it." Vanessa returned to arranging the broccoli florets. "He's been talking about Troy all week."

Cassandra swallowed hard. Convincing her parents she and Troy didn't belong together might be more difficult than she thought. Not that it wasn't obvious they came from different worlds, had different goals. Maybe if he were still a farmer from Missouri, but he was a venture capitalist from San Francisco. Talk about repeating similar patterns. Her parents would have to realize the relationship would never work. If only Troy didn't want them to act like the perfect couple. "Do you want me to do anything?"

"Why don't you get the beers? I chilled some mugs in the freezer."

Chilled mugs? Cassandra stared at the bowls and pans in the sink. The scent of the cooling brownies lingered in the air. With custom cabinets and state-of-the-art appliances, the kitchen was a cook's dream. The remodeling job had been a present for her mother last year, after their longtime cook retired but Vanessa never had any interest in cooking. Her parents hired a caterer when they had company, even for Christmas dinner, and usually ate out or had their meals delivered. When had her mother turned into Martha Stewart?

Cassandra grabbed two mugs from the freezer and set them on the counter. Opening the refrigerator, she saw three different brands of bottled beer. "Does Dad prefer a specific kind?"

"Any one will do, but give them both the same brand. I'm sure your father will want to know Troy's opinion about the beer."

"When did Dad start drinking beer?" She opened the bottles. "I thought he only liked Scotch."

"Your father's always liked beer, but he enjoys the ones from microbreweries best. He's got a database of all the brands he's tasted." Vanessa laughed. "He likes one so much he's going to invest in it."

As Cassandra started to pour the beer, her mother stopped her. "Make sure you tilt the glass. Your father hates too much head."

Her father, a beer connoisseur? It was hard for Cassandra to believe, but she poured the beer as her mother suggested. "What are you making?"

"A light snack." Vanessa wiped her hands on the apron. "Stuffed mushroom caps, a vegetable tray and brownies."

Cassandra eyed the chocolate batter on a wooden spoon. "I thought you gave up cooking."

"I did, but I missed it." Vanessa removed her apron. "Your father had this wonderful kitchen remodeled for me so I figured I should at least attempt to get a small return on his investment."

Cassandra grabbed the spoon and licked the chocolate off. "Dad must be happy."

Vanessa nodded. "But he's gaining weight again."

"I'm sure the beer isn't helping."

"It isn't," her mother agreed, but didn't seem to mind as long as Dixon was happy.

"Thanks for going to all of this trouble, Mom."

"I want Troy to feel like this is his home, too. After all, he's practically family."

Practically family. The key word was "practically." "Well, almost."

Vanessa sighed. "There's something you should know, Cassandra."

Her mother sounded so serious. Cassandra narrowed her eyes. "What?"

"Your father and I have had several discussions about this weekend's sleeping arrangements."

This, she could handle. Cassandra smiled. "Let Troy have the guest room. I'll sleep in my room."

"That's what your father said, but I don't want Troy to think we're, well, prudes."

"Troy won't think that." Cassandra tucked a lock of hair behind her ear. "This is your house and while we're staying here we'll follow your rules."

"You sound so grown-up, sweetheart." Vanessa smiled. "I'm so happy you found someone like him. I don't want to do anything to, uh—"

"Screw it up."

"In a manner of speaking, yes." Her mother looked uncomfortable at the choice of words. "You're old enough to make your own decisions."

Now that Cassandra had found an acceptable fiancé, she could make her own decisions without parental interference. It boggled her mind. She ran a successful bookstore, paid all her bills, visited her dentist every six months and still received no respect. But bring home a handsome male and bam—she was an adult. Maybe she could market the idea of make-believe fiancés to other women.

"I don't want to cause problems between you and Troy," her mother said finally. "When your father spent the weekend with my parents for the first time, he was so nervous I thought he would sweat to death. Troy needs to have you close to him."

Her mother was usually more direct. "What are you saying?"

"The two of you can share your room."

Cassandra almost dropped the beer bottle. "But—"

Vanessa raised an eyebrow. "I thought you would be happy."

"I'm shocked," Cassandra said, unable to believe what was happening. She didn't want to share her bedroom with a stranger. Not that Troy was strange. He was cute. She just didn't know him well enough. She knew him well enough to call him her fiancé, but not to share her room with him. Oh, no. Cassandra clutched the counter. There had to be a way out. "What about Daddy? I don't want to cause problems between the two of you."

"I can handle your father," Vanessa said with confidence. "It's time he realized you're not ten years old anymore."

"Really, Mom. Troy and I don't mind. We talked about it on the drive down. We don't want to do anything to make you and Dad feel uncomfortable."

"We are fine with the arrangements."

Cassandra didn't know what to say. What would Troy say? Her lips tightened.

"Wipe your face, dear, you have chocolate on it."

Chocolate was the least of her worries, but she wiped her face with a paper towel anyway. "Thanks."

"One more thing," Vanessa said. "I do hope you've been practicing safe sex."

"Mother, really," Cassandra said, wondering how many times her mother would shock her tonight.

"There are some nasty diseases out there, Cassandra."

"I know, it's—" She was at a loss for words. Sex wasn't a topic she wanted to discuss with her mother.

"Just take care of yourself, okay?"

She gritted her teeth. "Okay."

Vanessa grabbed the platters. "Let's take the food out."

Stunned, Cassandra picked up the two mugs of beer. How difficult had it been for her conservative mother to take on her even more conservative father over the issue of sleeping arrangements and to bring up the subject of safe sex with her own daughter? Very, she realized. "Mom. Thanks for being so understanding."

"I was young once, Cassandra."

"You're still young, Mom."

At midnight, Dixon told everyone it was time for bed. As Cassandra picked up her bag from the entryway, she couldn't believe how smoothly the last three hours had gone. Every bit of her mother's delicious food was gone, including the pan of brownies. Troy seemed at ease around her parents, almost like one of the family. His arm felt so comfortable around her, Cassandra could almost believe they were engaged. And her parents' delighted smiles told her they didn't suspect a thing.

Vanessa led the way upstairs, and Cassandra followed. Each step sent her closer to the impending doom. As her mother opened the door to her room, Cassandra's stomach knotted. She would have to share a bedroom and a bed with Troy.

As Vanessa turned on the light, her shoulders slumped. "Dixon," she yelled.

He ran up the stairs, gently pushing Cassandra aside. "Yes, dear?"

"What have you done?" Vanessa didn't sound pleased.

"Nothing, dear."

"I can't believe you did this," Vanessa mumbled to Dixon. "You're going to mess this up."

Cassandra couldn't believe the indignant tone of her mother's whispers. Eager to see what was happening, she nudged her way past her parents and into her bedroom. She couldn't believe her eyes when she saw the two twin beds.

*Thank you, Daddy.* She held back her laughter. Her mother might have won the battle, but her father had won the war.

"Where is Cassandra's bed?" Vanessa asked.

"Cassie's mattress was old and lumpy, dear. She needed a new mattress, so I bought her a new one."

"You bought two new ones."

"They were on sale," Dixon said. "Two for the price of one."

Her mother stared at the purple-and-white striped comforters. "Where did you get the bedding?"

"They were on sale, too."

"Well, at least they match." Vanessa shrugged. "I hope you don't mind, Cassandra."

She didn't mind at all. Cassandra smiled at her good fortune. "This is fine, isn't it, Troy?"

Troy entered the room and set his bag on a bed. "Yes."

"Good night, kids," Dixon said. "These walls are thin, so let us know if we're keeping you awake."

His comment earned him an elbow jab from Vanessa. On his way out of the room, Dixon left the door ajar.

Cassandra smiled, trying to ease her embarrassment. "My father isn't known for his subtlety."

"At least I know where I stand." Troy flashed her

a charming grin. "If I touch you, he'll come after me with a shotgun."

Cassandra laughed. "You'd better keep your hands to yourself, then."

"I assume we're sharing this room." Troy didn't sound too happy with the idea.

"Yes, and you can blame my mother. At least my father had sense enough to buy twin beds. He's the greatest, isn't he?"

"What used to be in here?"

"A full-size antique four-poster bed." She left out the romantic description of the carved oak headboard. She didn't want to scare Troy off, nor did she want to inspire any romantic dreams of her own.

"A full?"

She nodded, understanding his concern. "It would have been crowded. You don't know how happy I am to see these twin beds."

"I'm relieved," Troy said. "I wish I could thank your father."

Cassandra wished he didn't sound so happy. Would sharing a bed with her be that miserable? Not that she wanted to, but his obvious relief stung a little. She might not be a cover model, but plenty of men asked her out. She just never said yes.

"I still can't believe they're letting us share a room."

"As I said that was my mother's idea, but my father drew the line at us sharing a bed."

"I'm not sure he'd let us do that once we were married."

"You're probably right," Cassandra said, wondering what it would be like to share a bed with Troy. Tall and well built, he would take up the entire bed and be a blanket hog. Still, his body could keep her warm.

Troy rubbed his eyes. "Not that we'll ever find out."

"Of course not." She ignored the twinge of regret. It was for the best. She wasn't interested in anything about Troy McKnight. And as soon as this pretend engagement was over, she would never set eyes on him again. "Do you want to use the bathroom first?"

"No, you can." Troy opened his bag and tossed her a shirt. "Here."

She stared at the white T-shirt in her hand. "What's this for?"

"Did you bring pajamas?"

"No."

"Wear it."

The tone of his voice bothered her. "Are you always this bossy?"

"Only when my sanity's at stake."

His comment threw her. She wasn't sure whether to take his remarks as a compliment or not. Remember he's rigid and predictable. No spontaneity, no adventure. Maybe she could lighten him up a bit. "Were you a Boy Scout, Troy?"

"Eagle Scout," he said.

As Cassandra stepped into the bathroom, she winked at him. "Does that mean you're always prepared?"

The door to the bathroom opened. Cassie stepped out, carrying her clothes. She wore his T-shirt, but nothing else. The hem of the shirt brushed the top of her thighs. Her breasts pressed against the thin fabric. She shouldn't hide such luscious curves under all those baggy clothes of hers. Troy sucked in a breath. And he should have brought the flannel pajamas his mother had given him last Christmas.

"It's all yours," Cassie said.

And he wanted it, all of it. His groin tightened.

"There are clean towels in the cabinet."

She'd meant the bathroom, of course. He forced his gaze from her never-ending legs. "Okay."

Grabbing his shaving kit and a pair of shorts, Troy walked into the bathroom and slammed the door. How in the world would he sleep with Cassie a mere three feet away? He gritted his teeth.

He'd been without a woman too long.

Cassie might not be his type, but she was sexy and nothing like the career-driven women he dated. Or would date if he could ever afford the time. That must be his problem—he hadn't been dating anyone. It wasn't Cassie who was driving him crazy; it could be any attractive woman. That's why he found someone so not-his-type appealing. Troy splashed his face with cold water.

At least he understood his physical reaction to her. Now, he could forget about it. Besides, he wasn't here to appease his sexual desires, or frustrations in this case. He was here only because he had to be here. His current state of celibacy didn't matter. His future as a venture capitalist did. He'd been handed a golden opportunity to spend time with Dixon Daniels—one Troy wouldn't waste on hormones and the need for immediate gratification.

When Troy returned to the bedroom, Cassie was sitting cross-legged on the floor with her back to him. She still had the flower tucked behind her ear. He studied her, ignoring the way the T-shirt had inched up on her creamy thighs. Cassie glanced back, but didn't say a word.

She must have been meditating. "I'm sorry if I interrupted you."

"You didn't." She rose from the floor. "I'm done."

"Do you meditate every night?"

"Not every night." She crawled into the bed closest to her. "But it helps keep the stress levels down."

Troy couldn't imagine what stress she could have unless the stars and planets were out of alignment.

Cassie covered herself with a comforter. "Have you ever tried yoga?"

"Uh, no."

"Works wonders especially after long hours at the office."

"I'm not the yoga type."

She stared at him. "No, you're not."

The certainty in her voice bothered him, so did her slight grin. Not that he cared what Cassie thought.

"The light switch is on your right."

As he was about to turn off the light, he saw a white lace bra lying on top of her yellow sweater. Troy blinked and flicked off the switch. It was going to be a long night.

He got into bed. He hadn't slept in a twin-size bed since college. His feet hung over the edge. "Good night, Cassie."

"Good night, Troy."

Unable to sleep, he stared at the ceiling. He thought he saw stars. When he found the Big Dipper, he knew that he had. "Cassie."

"What?"

"There are stars on the ceiling."

"Yes."

He searched the fluorescent stars, locating Orion. "Why are there stars?"

"I've always loved to stargaze."

"Me, too. Growing up on the farm, I got spoiled. With no city lights to interfere, you can always see a sky full of stars." Troy searched the ceiling for other constellations. He found Andromeda and Eridanus. "You still haven't told me why there are stars on your ceiling."

"When I was little, I would lie on the grass in the backyard and stare at the stars with my planisphere in hand. One winter it got so cold, my mother thought I'd catch pneumonia. My father had the glow-in-the dark stars put on the ceiling so I could stay warm while I scanned the sky for constellations."

Troy located the Pleiades. "He did a great job."

"He hired a couple of astronomers to do it, so it's pretty accurate. For a bedroom ceiling that is."

He couldn't imagine what it would be like to have Vanessa and Dixon Daniels as parents. He couldn't imagine spending the money to stick fluorescent stars on a ceiling. Someday...

"My mother hated us going out in the winter, too." Troy remembered how he looked like the Michelin Man by the time his mother finished dressing him for an evening of stargazing in the chilly night air. "But on the clearest and coldest night you could always see what seemed like a million stars in the sky."

Cassie sighed. "Sounds like heaven. Why did you leave?"

"I got tired of living on a farm. I watched my parents grow old worrying about money, about the weather, about grain prices." About how to pay for their children's college education, their own retirement and groceries. It wasn't fair. His father was only fifty-two, but had lines of worry etched on his forehead.

"But aren't there a few pluses to living on a farm?" Cassie asked. "No crowds, no traffic, lots of open spaces."

True, but Troy didn't want to live hand-to-mouth or harvest-to-harvest. The only way to get what he wanted meant leaving the farm. A sacrifice, perhaps, but one he'd make again. Cassie grew up rich. She wouldn't understand his reasons, understand how his family still struggled though he helped out as much as he could. "There are pros and cons. Floods and droughts. It isn't an easy life."

"I always thought it would be fun." Cassie sounded as if she disapproved of his reasons.

"It's a lot of work."

A star fell from the ceiling.

"Did you see that, Troy?"

He squinted, trying to focus in the darkness. "What?"

"A falling star," she said with childlike excitement. "Make a wish."

Wishing on a plastic star? Troy rolled his eyes. She probably tossed coins into fountains, too. "It's not a real star, Cassie."

"So? It can't hurt. Don't be so unimaginative." She paused. "Did you make a wish?"

"Yes." He had wished for a BMW. It didn't take a Ph.D. to realize she wouldn't take no for an answer. And he wasn't unimaginative. "What did you wish for, Cassie?"

"If I tell you, it won't come true," she said. "I've

always thought you could learn a lot about a person by knowing what they wished for.''

Troy wondered what he could learn from Cassie's wish. She probably wished for world peace or an end to hunger.

''I'm happy you made a wish. I was beginning to think you were a total stick-in-the-mud.'' She rolled over. ''Good night, Troy.''

''Good night.''

He stared at the ceiling. Another star fell. He made a wish. No way was he a so-called ''stick-in-the-mud.'' But…

Terrific, he thought, feeling himself tense.

Did wishes tell something about a person? What did it tell about him? He'd made a wish and it shocked the hell out of him. He should have wished for a partnership or his own company, but he hadn't.

Troy had wished for Cassie.

# 4

The warmth of the morning sun hit Cassandra's face. The smell of freshly brewed coffee lingered in the air. It must be time to get up. She stretched her arms over her head, then slowly opened her eyes. Unbelievably she felt well rested.

With Troy three feet away wearing only a pair of gray athletic shorts, she couldn't believe she'd fallen asleep. But she had.

She'd dreamed of making love with a man with a muscular chest and curly brown hair. A sensual dream that nearly overwhelmed her, leaving her hot and bothered. Too bad the emphasis wasn't on the "bothered." She didn't want to dream about a man; she wanted nothing to do with men.

But it meant nothing. It was a dream. Thank goodness.

One night down, one to go. Then she could say goodbye to her fiancé for the weekend. Cassandra smiled. She glanced over at Troy, but he wasn't there. His empty bed had already been made.

Troy and her parents. Alone.

Panicked, Cassandra bolted upright. She gripped the edge of the comforter. One tiny foul-up and her intelligent parents would figure out the engagement was a scam. The whole thing would blow up in her face. She could handle the consequences, but what about Troy? Just because she'd made a mess of her life didn't mean she needed to wreck his, too.

She jumped out of bed and raced for the door. Halfway down the hall, she skidded to a stop.

Pants. She needed pants.

Running back to her room, Cassandra saw a pair of gray shorts sitting on Troy's bed. She tossed them on and pulled the drawstring tight so they wouldn't fall off.

*Let me get there in time. Please.*

Cassandra ran down the stairs, picking up the pace when she heard voices coming from the kitchen. Her heart pounded. Her mother, her father and Troy. What a nightmare!

Why hadn't she set an alarm clock?

Taking a deep breath, she calmed herself. At this point, she could only hope everything was going well.

Stepping into the kitchen, she crossed her fingers behind her back. Her father and Troy sat in the breakfast nook. The royal blue of Troy's polo shirt intensified the color of his eyes. The power of his gaze took her breath away.

The expression on Troy's smiling face told her what she needed to know. No need to worry. Things were going fine.

"Good morning, Cassandra." Vanessa closed the waffle iron and wiped her hands on the front of her yellow apron. "You're up early this morning."

Cassandra glanced at the microwave clock. "What time is it?"

"Seven-thirty," Dixon said. She noticed the "isn't

it sweet'' look in his twinkling blue eyes. If he only knew… ''Couldn't you sleep, Cassie?''

She combed her fingers through her messy hair. ''No sense sleeping the day away, Dad.''

Dixon laughed. ''Troy, you must be a good influence. When Cassie was a teenager, she used to wake up around noon.''

''Now, she never gets up before nine,'' Troy said with another smile that showed his perfect white teeth. He picked up his mug and drank.

How did he know what time she got up? Cassandra found herself staring at him again. She frowned. Why was she having such a difficult time not looking at him? His hair, of course. Troy's hair curled in damp ringlets that begged to be played with.

''Did you sleep well, beautiful?'' Troy asked.

Cassandra hesitated. He'd called her beautiful. Not that he meant it. ''Yes, so well I didn't hear you get up.''

''You didn't?''

Cassandra ignored his playful grin. ''No.''

She had been too busy dreaming about him. *And what a dream!* She got worked up just thinking about it. She should have asked the nerd sitting next to Troy in the microbrewery to be her fiancé instead. Troy was too gorgeous for his own good. And hers, too.

''You said good morning to me.''

''I did?'' Her mind drew a blank. She remembered only her dream of making love to a man with unruly brown hair, a man who looked remarkably like Troy. She hadn't made a pass at him, had she? Of course not. She didn't sleepwalk or anything as far as she knew.

Troy nodded and set his coffee cup down. "Come over here, so I can say good morning properly."

Cassandra blushed. She glanced at her parents and caught their pleased exchange. Both wore wide smiles. They thought she and Troy were a couple. She should be happy; she was pulling it off.

As Cassandra approached Troy, her pulse picked up speed. *This is an act. This isn't real.* She repeated the mantra in her mind.

Troy pulled her onto his lap. He caressed her cheek with his fingertips, sending a pleasant shiver down her spine. He winked, then kissed her, his mouth warm and wet. He tasted like French Roast coffee. Much too soon, he ended the kiss. For a moment, his lips hovered near hers. His breath fanned her mouth like a soft feather and Cassandra wanted more.

"Good morning, my love." Troy leaned back, breaking the spell.

*This means nothing.* The kiss was merely for show, but her body tingled, a little unclear of the point. Craving more, every nerve ending pulsated with sensation, with electricity. Goose bumps covered her bare legs and arms.

It's the cold, Cassandra rationalized. But she wasn't cold. In fact, she felt downright feverish. Must be the heat radiating from Troy's body. Men were always warm. Of course, that was it. She scooted over to the empty chair next to Troy, who placed his arm around her shoulder. Be careful. Be very careful.

Vanessa set a plate with a steaming Belgian waffle in front of Troy. "Would you like strawberries and whipped cream?"

"No, thanks." Troy removed his arm from Cassandra's shoulder and placed his napkin in his lap. "Butter and syrup are fine."

"How about some coffee, Cassie?" Dixon asked.

Maybe a cup of iced coffee would cool her down. She nixed the idea. She needed to keep everything as normal as possible. "I'd love a cup."

Dixon filled her mug, then added a dash of milk and a little sugar, the way she liked it.

"Thanks, Dad." Cassandra took a sip. The coffee tasted like Troy. And his kiss. Something she didn't want to think about. Not now, not ever.

*You haven't been kissed in over a year. That's all it is. You didn't even like it. Forget the kiss.* With resolve, Cassandra set her cup on the table.

Vanessa placed a plate in front of her. "Here's your waffle, sweetheart."

Piled with strawberries, whipped cream and chocolate sauce, the waffle, her favorite breakfast food, looked delicious. So how come she would rather have another taste of Troy instead? "Thanks, Mom."

Troy raised an eyebrow. "You like chocolate sauce on your waffles?"

"Yes," she said. "Among other things."

"I like peanut butter and syrup on French toast."

"So does Cassie." Dixon smiled as if he'd made another million. "Vanessa, did you hear that? They both like peanut butter on their French toast."

Her father might be pleased, but liking peanut butter and syrup wouldn't be much of a foundation for a marriage. He would realize it soon enough. She and Troy were unsuited for each other. He wore Italian silk suits and leather shoes; she wore one hundred percent cotton and sandals. He worked to make money; she worked to enjoy her passion—books.

They had nothing in common. Nothing. As soon as they stopped pretending, it would be crystal clear to both of her parents. Peanut butter be damned.

As Cassandra took a bite of her waffle, she noticed her father wore his golf attire—a purple shirt, an argyle sweater and green pants. "What's your tee-time, Dad?"

"Nine o'clock." Dixon leaned against the back of his chair. "Troy and I are having lunch at the lodge after we finish."

Daddy and Troy.

Alone.

No way.

She couldn't let them go without her. What if Troy said something and Dixon discovered the truth? Troy's career would be ruined, and she would have to put up with her parents' endless advice and match-making. Or worse, what if her father believed they were as perfect a couple as they pretended to be? Dixon needed to see them together; he needed to understand why they shouldn't get married. This was too complicated.

"Mind if I join you?" She flashed Dixon her cutest smile. It had been fail-safe when she was growing up.

"Don't you remember what happened the last time I took you?" Dixon laughed. "Troy, whatever you do, don't let Cassie play golf. She loses too many balls."

*So much for being cute.* "The balls are small and I don't understand why there are so many ponds and sand traps between the holes," Cassandra said. Why anyone would want to pay all that money and suffer all that frustration was beyond her. Time for a new tactic. "I won't play, but let me drive the cart, Daddy."

"No."

She slapped her palm against the table. "I'm a good driver."

"You don't own a car, Cassie."

She glanced at Troy, willing him to help her. He shrugged. What kind of a fiancé was he? He was making her angry. She would have to talk to him about what was expected.

"I'll caddy." Unwilling to give up without a fight, she rubbed her fingers on her fork and hoped for inspiration. "I'm good with numbers, I can keep score."

Dixon narrowed his eyes. She ran the risk of ruining her own plans with all her good intentions. Her father would see right through her. She hated golf, and he knew it.

"Honey, I know you want to be with Troy, but your mother has a special day planned for you." Dixon's tone softened. "You wouldn't want to disappoint her, would you?"

She saw the expectant look in Vanessa's eyes. A rush of panic, then guilt, hit Cassandra like a stack of Stephen King novels falling on her head. She didn't want to hurt her mother, but how much was it going to cost to make her happy? Cassandra had already created a mythical fiancé to stop the matchmaking. She had brought home a pseudofiancé. What next, a pretend wedding? Or worse yet, the real thing? "No, I'm sure Mom and I will have a great time."

"Oh, we will," Vanessa said, her hazel eyes sparkling. "Remember the last time."

Yes, Cassandra remembered spending a day at a trendy spa—the beauty salon from hell. She'd spent hours convincing a hairdresser named Jean-Paul she not only liked the length of her hair, but the color, too. She clenched her fork. "What are we going to do?"

Vanessa's eyes widened. "It's a surprise, but it's going to be so much fun. You'll love it."

Cassandra suppressed a groan. More likely, she would hate it. Her mother and Emily had a different definition of fun than she had. Being primped and pampered didn't appeal to Cassandra.

Not that she had a choice today.

Might as well make the best of it. Cassandra bit into a forkful of her waffle. She was tough. She was resilient. As long as Jean-Paul and her hair weren't involved, she could handle anything.

Troy took one step into the bedroom, then stopped. He thought Cassie would have been showered and dressed by the time he finished eating another waffle.

He'd been wrong. Dead wrong. Damn.

Cassie stood in the middle of the room, fumbling with the zipper on the back of her black flower-print dress. The strap of her black bra contrasted with her velvety white skin. He stiffened. "I'll be back in a minute."

"You don't have to go," she said, turning. "I want to talk to you."

Talk? How about another kiss? She had looked cuddly sexy coming to breakfast all sleep-rumpled in his clothes. She looked plain sexy now. "Do you need help?"

"Help? Now you offer help." Cassandra sighed. "I needed your help downstairs."

"What are you talking about?"

"I wanted you to convince my father I should go

with you today.'' She struggled with the zipper. ''But you said nothing, nada, zilch.''

''What did you want me to say? Let Cassie drive the cart?'' He put his hand on her slim waist. ''You're going to ruin your dress. Let me help.''

Cassie held her single braid. It reminded him of a thick, gold rope. Rapunzel would have hair like this. As he reached for her zipper, his hand brushed against her back and she tensed. Whatever chemistry existed between them, Cassie must feel it, too.

Troy ignored the graceful curve of her neck and the softness of her skin. He concentrated on the zipper that wouldn't budge and tugged harder until he freed it from the edge of the fabric. He zipped her up, then let go so he wouldn't give in to the urge to pull it back down. ''All done. I'll be downstairs.''

''Thanks, but we still need to talk.'' She placed her hands on her hips. ''Couldn't you tell I wanted to go golfing?''

''Yes, but…'' He hesitated, knowing she wouldn't like the truth.

''But—''

''I didn't want you to go.''

''What?''

''Not so loud,'' he said, worried what Dixon might hear through the walls.

''Why didn't you want me to go?''

''Cassie, things are going well.''

''Things are not going well. Did you see the look in my parents' eyes?''

Troy nodded. ''They were smiling so much I thought I was in the middle of a toothpaste commercial. They think we're the perfect couple.''

''Exactly. See the problem?''

"I don't," Troy said. "We decided to act like an engaged couple. You'd get your parents off your back, I get my partnership."

"Engaged couple, yes." Cassie plopped on her bed. "But not soul mates destined to be together forever."

"You're overreacting. We've been here less than twenty-four hours. There's no way Dixon and Vanessa could believe we're destined to be together, forever."

"I think they do." She tapped her foot against the floor. "We've got to stop our happy couple routine or I'll have to live the rest of my life hearing about Troy McKnight—the other one who got away."

*The other one?* Not that he would ask. Not with the pained expression on Cassie's face. "It won't be that bad."

"You don't know my parents."

"I still don't understand what this has to do with golfing."

"Men," she muttered, glancing at the ceiling. "Don't you see? The more time we spend together, the easier it will be to show my parents we shouldn't be engaged."

He had too much riding on this to blow it. "We decided to get through the weekend by acting like an engaged couple. We were going to worry about breaking up later. We can't change our plans now."

"Haven't you heard anything I've said?"

"I heard you, but I disagree."

"So you're not going to convince my father to let me come with you?"

"No, you're going with your mother." Troy wished Cassie would smile. "I want to spend time with your father. Alone, if possible. He's a great contact to have and I might learn some tricks of the trade. Maybe he

can teach me some things that will ensure my partnership.''

''I should have known.'' She rubbed her forehead.
''All you care about is how this affects you and your
career.''

''That's not true.''

''Yes, it is.'' Cassie narrowed her eyes. ''You can't
do anything to risk your precious partnership.''

''I've never hidden my reasons from you.''

Silence.

''Listen, Cassie, your parents don't need us to show
them we aren't the prefect couple. It's obvious we
don't belong together.''

''I'll say it's obvious. Two people couldn't be more
different,'' she said. ''You're much too yuppie for
me.''

''You're too spontaneous for me.''

''At least I wouldn't use anybody and anything to
get ahead.''

''Please don't overreact.''

''I'm being 'spontaneous.''' She frowned. ''Unlike
you, Mr. Rigid. I bet you have a plan to get you where
you want to be.''

Troy did—his master plan. And it was working. Or
had been. Until he met Cassie.

''A partnership at thirty,'' she said. ''Your first million by thirty-two. Retirement at thirty-five.''

''Forty.'' She had guessed all the milestones, but
missed the ages by a couple of years.

''Where does happiness play into your plan,
Troy?''

''When I succeed, I'll be happy.''

Cassie rolled her eyes. ''You're just like…''

Her father, Troy hoped. ''I'm like who?''

"Eric."

The day couldn't get much worse.

Her argument with Troy had set the tone. Nothing resolved, nothing gained except irritation. Cassandra should have taken that as an omen and crawled back into bed.

She had come down on him hard, maybe too hard. But he didn't realize how easily this situation could start spinning out of control. She didn't want them to crash and burn.

Then came lunch with her mother who couldn't stop talking about Troy and acted like his personal publicist. So much so that Cassandra had lost her appetite. She didn't need to be reminded about Troy's striking eyes and charming smile over her Caesar salad with marinated grilled chicken breast.

And now this.

Cassandra stood in a strapless bra contraption and hoop slip. Staring at a three-paneled, gilded mirror, she tried to decide if she looked as silly as she felt. Although she could barely breathe, her bustline looked great. At least that's what Ginger Soren, the owner of Bridal Couture, told her. And she should know.

In her knockout hot pink suit and matching pumps, Ginger looked like a runway model with her blush hollowed cheekbones. Thick, black eyeliner emphasized her sea green eyes. Her coiffured hair had been shellacked into place with hair spray. Yes, Ginger was the definition of fashionable. At least as far as wedding gown salons went.

Ginger carried a monstrous pile of white silk and ruffles. "Try this one."

Cassandra eyed the gown cautiously. "I don't know."

"This one will look better than the mermaid gowns you tried on earlier, I promise," Ginger said.

"Cassandra," Vanessa said in a patient tone. "Why don't you try it?"

"Okay."

Ginger helped Cassandra into the gown. An avalanche of tulle cascaded over her head. Finally it was on. Ginger buttoned the back.

"Oh, my." She clapped her hands. "You look as though you stepped from a page in a bride magazine."

Horrified, Cassandra stared at her reflection. She looked like Scarlett O'Hara wearing the gaudy curtain dress. Cassandra had nothing against Southern belles or the plantation-style gowns, but this was ridiculous. The puffy sleeves made her look like a linebacker for the 49ers. The thousands of tiny sequins and beads sewn on the bodice sparkled like a neon sign on the Las Vegas strip. She wanted to strip it off and run like hell, but she was trapped.

The dress shimmered under the light of the chandelier hanging overhead. The blue carpet accented the whiteness of the fabric. As a combination, it was almost blinding. A disco ball was more subdued than this gown.

Ginger handed her a pair of white gloves. "Try these on."

*This was too much.* Cassandra wanted to go home. She wanted to run away and forget about her family and about Troy. She glanced at Vanessa, who motioned for her to try on the gloves.

"What do you think?" Ginger asked, visibly pleased with the overall effect.

"It's a little too, uh…" Cassandra couldn't find words, polite ones, to describe it.

Vanessa's assessing gaze took in every detail of the elaborate gown. "It's beautiful, but I think a simpler bodice would suit you better. The sleeves almost overwhelm you."

"We can fix the sleeves," Ginger said.

*No one could fix these sleeves.*

"There's something else about the dress," Vanessa said. "I know, it reminds me of the gown Emily wore."

No wonder Cassandra hated it.

"This gown is by the same designer." Ginger pursed her lips.

"It's lovely," Vanessa reassured. "But my daughters have different tastes. Like Waterford and Orrefors."

"I understand." Ginger smiled. "Let me get you out of this dress, then I'll bring more for you to try on."

After Ginger left the dressing room, Cassandra frowned. Her mother might be reasonable about the wedding gown, but she was still pushing. Pushing Cassandra to get married. Pushing her to do the right things with her life. Pushing her to be something she wasn't.

"I should have been more clear with Ginger," Vanessa said. "I'm sure she assumed you'd want a gown like Emily's."

"Like I'd want anything to remind me of her wedding."

"Sweetheart, I know you are still upset over Emily marrying Eric, but it was for the best. Eric was not the man for you. He wouldn't have made you happy.

You've got such a wonderful future ahead of you with Troy.'' Vanessa's eyes sparkled. ''Can't you forget about the past?''

If only Cassandra could forget, but it wasn't easy to forget the pain—the pain of having her heart ripped out. The betrayal still stung. She found it difficult to trust anyone. How was she supposed to forget and put it behind her?

''Once we find you a wedding dress, I'm sure you'll feel better,'' Vanessa said.

Cassandra rubbed her temples, trying to stop the headache threatening to erupt. This was too much. The dress. The engagement. It was all a charade. Everything. She should put a stop to it right now.

''What if we forget about finding a dress?'' Cassandra asked. ''I could wear a toga. In fact, we could have all of the guests wear togas. I could make a wreath out of fig leaves—''

''Cassandra, really,'' Vanessa said. ''Could you imagine your father in a toga? Just the thought.''

''It was only an idea, Mom.'' At least Cassandra had tried. And she liked the idea of Troy in a toga with nothing underneath. What was wrong with her? She shouldn't think about Troy that way, even though he was the most gorgeous man she'd ever seen and the best kisser she'd ever kissed. Bottom line, he was like Eric Wainwright—same ambition, same drive, same everything.

She should have never told her mother she was engaged. Yes, it had seemed like the perfect solution to stop her parents from meddling and matchmaking, but now Cassandra wasn't so sure. If only her parents understood she didn't mind being alone. She knew something they didn't. Being alone was better than the alternative—having her heart broken again.

Ginger returned with three dresses. The first was an elegant sleeveless silk ballroom gown with a lace-covered bodice. It reminded Cassandra of a dress Audrey Hepburn would have worn. The next dress was short-sleeved with a small bow at the sweetheart neckline. Simple yet charming. She liked both dresses.

"I think you'll like this one the best." Ginger helped Cassandra into the next gown and buttoned up the back. "I call it my English garden wedding dress."

Cassandra stared at herself in the mirror. The dress was gorgeous. Made of silk with alternating wide stripes of white and ivory, the dress had a small bow on each sleeve and a larger, matching bow in the back.

On the front of the plain, tight-fitting bodice, six round fabric-covered buttons narrowed in a V to the baroque waist. No lace, no beading, no pearls. Perfect.

Vanessa dabbed her eyes with a tissue. "Oh, Cassandra."

"It's made to resemble an old-fashioned design, but the textured fabric gives it a modern flair." Ginger placed her right hand on her hip. "I think this dress makes more of a statement than the other two."

Cassandra looked like a bride; she felt like a bride. Not even the dress she had purchased to wear for her wedding with Eric made her feel this way. Thinking about the other dress dimmed her excitement, but only for a few seconds. This was the dress she wanted to be married in.

"If you don't like the striped fabric, we could have the dress made with plain silk. I'll go find a headpiece to match." Ginger walked around a corner.

"What do you think?" Vanessa asked.

"I like the stripes."

"Me, too," Vanessa said, much to Cassandra's surprise. She thought her mother would prefer the more traditional fabric.

Wearing this gown, Cassandra could imagine herself walking down the aisle. Plain, yet elegant and not completely traditional. Ginger was right. It could have been worn a hundred years ago in the English countryside. Cassandra imagined a wreath of fresh flowers in her hair. She couldn't wait for Troy to see her. He would love the dress, except...

Troy would never see her in this dress.

"Do you like the gown?" Vanessa asked.

Disappointed with herself, disappointed with finding a dress she didn't need, Cassandra nodded. She felt like a deflated balloon that had popped itself by floating too high in the sky.

Time to get out of here. She needed to get out of the dress before she fell in love with it any more. Where was Ginger? Cassandra tapped her foot impatiently, waiting for her to return.

How could this have happened?

Cassandra felt like a fraud; she was a fraud. She loved the dress, but she couldn't have it. She wasn't getting married; she was never getting married.

Catching a glimpse of her reflection, Cassandra blinked back a tear. She'd found the perfect dress— the perfect dress for a wedding that would never happen.

# 5

———◄———

Later that afternoon, Troy stood on a street corner watching Cassie get her face painted. He'd wanted to relax and hang out with Dixon, but Cassie had had other ideas. Grabbing his arm, she'd dragged him to his truck. She'd given him no explanation, just a smile. Standard operating procedure for Cassie.

But still…

Something was on her mind. He could tell by the way she gnawed on her lip. He assumed it had something to do with their talk earlier, but didn't ask. She'd talk to him when she was ready. Troy had figured that out about her.

Cassie had wanted to go to the beach, so he drove her there. They'd walked along the wet sand in bare feet, smelling the salty air and listening to the waves crash against the shore. She'd said little, another sign telling him something was wrong. Then, she'd wanted to go to the village. And here they were.

Cassie sat on a wooden stool. "Are you sure you don't want your face painted, Troy?" A woman, wearing a clown suit, painted two daisies on Cassie's left cheek.

"I think I'll pass." Face painting wasn't for him, but Carmel was. He could get used to this. A gentle breeze blew though a rainbow wind sock hanging outside a flower shop. Birds chirped from a nearby tree. Tourists strolled along the quaint streets, visiting the many galleries and trendy boutiques.

Someone giggled behind him. He glanced back. Three young girls waited in line to have their faces painted. They whispered to one another. He smiled. One of the girls, dressed in pink overalls, blushed and covered her mouth with her hands. She had curly blond hair—a little angel. All she needed was a pair of wings and a halo. Seeing her made Troy wonder what Cassie had looked like when she was younger. No doubt a real cutie with her heart-shaped face and baby blue eyes, like the little girl standing behind him.

Troy sighed. He hoped he had all boys when he had children. Girls would age a man, fast. Especially if they turned out to be anything like Cassie.

*Whoa. Where had that come from?*

He wanted a family, yes. But not now. And not with Cassie. She was attractive, but unconventional.

Not his type.

The perfect fiancée for a weekend, but not any longer. Troy knew what it took to get ahead. He needed a woman, make that a wife, who would be an asset to his career, not a novelty. Cassie wouldn't be content standing around and chatting politely at a cocktail party. She would probably pull out a deck of tarot cards and offer to do readings in order to liven things up.

Not the woman for him.

Sliding off the stool, Cassie handed the clown a five-dollar bill. With a big grin on her face, she turned toward him and struck a pose, giving him a perfect view of the daisies on her flushed cheek. The flowers matched the ones on her dress. "What do you think?"

She smiled. A good sign. "It's nice."

"Nice?" Cassie balked. Two little lines formed above the bridge of her nose. "I wonder how you would describe my tattoo?"

"You have a tattoo?" As he said the words, Troy wondered why he would be surprised. Nothing about her should surprise him. A tattoo. Cassie would have a flower. Wildflowers? A rose, perhaps? But where? The idea of finding it made him smile.

"Yes, don't you?" She made it sound like having a tattoo was the same as having pierced ears.

"Uh, no."

"You really need to spice up your life, Troy. You wouldn't want anyone to think you were boring."

Next to Cassie, anyone would seem bland. "My life is exciting enough."

"Suit yourself."

"So where is this tattoo of yours?"

She tilted her chin. "That's my secret. No one knows where it is except me."

"And the tattoo artist."

"Of course."

The seductive smile on Cassie's face intrigued Troy. He imagined trying to find her tattoo, but the image overwhelmed him. He needed to cool off. "Would you like to get an ice cream?"

"Sure. There's a place around the corner."

The ice-cream parlor was almost empty except for a family of four sitting in the corner. Cassie ordered a scoop of Rocky Road and a scoop of Chocolate Fudge Brownie on a sugar cone. Troy settled for a scoop of vanilla in a cup.

"Do you want to eat it here?" he asked.

"Yes." Cassie pointed to a round, marble table near the window. "I want to know about your day with my father."

Troy grabbed four napkins, handing three of them to Cassie before he sat at the table. "We had a great time."

"Details, Troy."

He ate a spoonful of his delicious-looking ice cream. Cool and tasty, just what he needed to forget Cassie, who was hot and tasty. "Details, huh?"

She nodded. "Don't leave anything out."

"Let's see, I lost the round so I bought lunch."

Her eyes widened. "My father let you buy? Wow."

Troy didn't consider buying lunch a big deal. He'd insisted on buying, but didn't tell her. "Dixon beat me, but he was upset over his score."

"He has a four handicap."

"Dixon said he was a hacker."

A drop of chocolate dribbled from Cassie's mouth. She licked her lips catching the chocolate with the pink tip of her tongue. "He plays at least three times a week."

"I was had." And Dixon wasn't the only one trying to take him. Troy wondered if Cassie was trying to drive him crazy.

He took a bite of his ice cream. Although tasty, it didn't do much to cool him down. Not with Cassie seductively licking her ice-cream cone, making him wonder what else she could be doing with her tongue. Talk about torture. He couldn't wait until she finished eating it. He should have suggested getting a soda. Somehow being around Cassie sent his normally rational mind askew.

"I wouldn't worry about it. You probably made his day." She wiped her mouth with a napkin. "What else did you do?"

"We ate lunch at the lodge. Then Dixon gave me a tour. Surprise, surprise. We ended up in a large banquet room. He hinted it would be a nice place for a wedding reception."

Although Dixon had been far from subtle in maneuvering him into the room, Troy had to give him credit. The elegant room with a hardwood dance floor and picture windows overlooking the golf course and the Pacific Ocean would be the perfect place for a wedding reception. Someday. When he found the right woman and was ready to get married. But not in the near future. Marriage wasn't part of his near-term plan.

"So did the two of you select a date for the wedding and reserve the room?" Cassie sounded annoyed, but he found it hard to take her seriously with daisies painted on her cheek and chocolate on her upper lip.

"No, but your father thought April would be a good month." Reaching over, Troy wiped her lip with his napkin. "You missed a spot."

"Thanks."

"I thought about what you said this morning," he admitted. He'd thought about it, especially after Dixon mentioned an opening at his company. "I don't buy the soul mates for eternity, but I think your parents are getting a little carried away."

"I told you so."

Troy deserved that, but she didn't have to be so smug. "Can't we share the blame? After all, we are in this together."

"I suppose." Cassie bit into the crunchy cone.

It wasn't much, but it would do…for now.

"After Dixon showed me the room, I mentioned I wanted a traditional church wedding, but you wanted to get married in your bare feet at the beach and have a shaman perform the ceremony."

"A shaman." She chuckled. "I'm so proud of you, sweetie. I can't believe you came up with that on your own."

"I can be creative when called upon."

"What did he say?"

Cassandra's smile tugged at his heart. Troy realized her comparison of him to Eric Wainwright must have been due more to emotion and the moment than the truth. "Dixon said the beach might be difficult. Women in high heels. But he didn't see a problem if you went barefoot."

"My father said that?"

Troy nodded, not mentioning Dixon thought Cassie's gown would cover her feet so it wouldn't matter whether she wore shoes or not.

"What about the shaman?"

Troy laughed. "He didn't see a problem with that, either."

"You're kidding me?"

"I wish I were."

"Please tell me you said something else."

"Well…"

She sighed. "Your sheepish grin tells me everything I need to know, Troy McKnight. Damn. You didn't say a word."

"Cassie—"

"You could've told my father I want you to quit your job and farm algae in Oregon."

"Like he'd believe that," Troy said. "I said all I

could. I didn't want to press the issue and be too obvious.''

''Why not?''

''We were having a good time.'' Besides, he felt as though he owed it to Dixon, who had taught him more during eighteen holes of golf than in one of Troy's business school classes. The career advice had been invaluable. ''I didn't want to spoil it.''

''You.'' Cassie threw one of her napkins at him. ''You're too nice.''

No, he wasn't nice. If he were nice he wouldn't be wishing he could have licked the chocolate off her face instead of wiping it off.

''Do you ever *not* play by the rules?'' she asked.

''Not if I can help it.''

''Hopeless. You're positively hopeless.''

''I'll take that as a compliment.''

''Go right ahead.''

He grinned. ''What about you? How was your day?''

Cassie rubbed her temples and groaned. ''My mother took me shopping for a wedding gown.''

Judging from her reaction, the shopping expedition did not go well. ''Did you find anything you liked?''

''As a matter of fact, I—'' She stopped herself, but she couldn't stop the blush reddening her cheeks. ''What are we doing? Before you know it, we'll be married and have a baby on the way.''

The dire sound of her voice made his smile widen. Marriage and a baby were a bit much. Though he liked the concept of how babies were made. ''I doubt that.''

She slammed her hands on the table. ''We need to do something drastic.''

Troy's gut tightened. Drastic to Cassie most likely

had a different definition than what he was used to. She was an extremist; he was a middle-of-the-road kind of guy. "I don't like the sound of drastic."

"I'm not saying we stage a revolution, but something along those lines." She tapped her fingertips on the table. "This is working out too well. My parents love you."

And Troy liked her parents. "We've already been through this, Cassie. We're halfway through the weekend. We're almost there."

She nodded. "But I didn't realize they'd be so excited about the wedding. You admitted this was getting a little out of control."

"Yes," he said, thinking about the possibility of working for Dixon one day. The job and Cassie would be a package deal. A package he couldn't begin to consider.

"I know you're worried about your career, but we can't forget about my sanity."

"I know."

Time for a reality check. Troy needed Cassie more than she needed him. Her parents' meddling was one thing, but his livelihood was on the line.

"This isn't easy, but we only have twenty-four more hours to go. We can get through this if we do it together." Her hesitation worried him. "Twenty-four more hours, Cassie. Think you can make it?"

"Yes," she said. "It's just… Oh, no."

"What?"

Her voice softened to a whisper. "Hold my hand and gaze lovingly into my eyes."

Troy assumed Cassie had a logical explanation for the sudden change. Until she lifted his hand and kissed each of his fingers. Obviously, she'd lost her mind.

He pulled his hand away, but she held it tighter. "What are you—"

"PDA in an ice-cream parlor," a female voice crooned, interrupting him. Troy turned. Emily led a frowning Eric to the table. "I can understand such a public display of affection from my sister, but Troy, really. I thought you were above that."

Cassie tightened her grip on his hand, then released it. "What are you doing here?"

"We were shopping and saw you in the window. I'm sure the entire village has been watching you."

The air filled with tension and did not feel sisterly. Cassie straightened in her chair. "I meant, why are you in Carmel?"

"Didn't mother tell you? I guess not from the expression on your face." Emily's tittering laughter filled the ice cream parlor. "Guess who's coming to dinner?"

To Cassandra's amazement, everyone behaved themselves at dinner. It reminded her of a meeting between warring nations trying to negotiate a peace treaty. No one wanted to say anything to offend the others so nothing interesting was said.

Her mother cooked a delicious prime rib, but Cassandra had a difficult time enjoying the food. With Emily and Eric monopolizing the conversation with their house hunting woes, Cassandra had too much time to think and daydream about Troy.

She pictured him standing in front of a flower-filled church waiting for her to walk down the aisle. Except for the flowers and bare feet, everything was wrong with the picture. It wasn't simply that Troy was wrong for her—he was—but so was the entire wedding picture.

She'd given up on love. She couldn't afford to love. Seeing Emily and Eric brought back the pain of finding them together in her apartment.

In her bed.

That was all Cassandra needed to remember. Love equaled hurt. With that in mind, it was easy to control her emotions.

Until she looked at Troy. Then she swallowed hard and reminded herself she didn't feel anything for him. Except…

The day of golfing in the sunshine had turned Troy's face a golden tan. The plaid of his oxford shirt intensified the striking blue of his eyes. He got more gorgeous by the minute. And that bothered the hell out of her.

She couldn't afford to think of Troy as anything other than her pretend fiancé, her fake fiancé. Anything more, she didn't want to deal with, wouldn't deal with. As soon as the weekend was over, she would be free. Free of her parents, free of Troy. But until then, she had to be one half of the perfect couple they'd created, one half of a lie.

After dinner, Cassandra followed everyone as they retreated into the living room to let their food digest and make room for dessert—devil's food cake.

One big happy family. Emily and Eric sat on one couch. Cassandra and Troy sat on the other. Dixon and Vanessa sat on chairs in the middle, playing referee and ensuring fair play.

*Show time.* Mindful of her sister's watchful eyes, Cassandra nestled against Troy. Leave it to Emily to decide something wasn't right with the engagement.

Her hints and innuendos had been less than subtle, but Emily would find only a happy, content engaged couple tonight.

As Troy draped his arm around her shoulder, Cassandra had trouble breathing. Her heart pounded so loudly; she glanced up at him to see if he'd noticed. She didn't think he had. His breathing was steady, and she could barely feel his heart beating against her shoulder. The fact he remained so calm as he played havoc with her vital signs irritated her. She wished Troy could share in her misery.

Dixon poured brandy into crystal snifters. "So have you decided about the dress, Cassie?"

The dress. Perfect, yes. But she didn't need another wedding gown. Come tomorrow night, she would no longer have a fiancé. "Not yet, Dad."

"I heard it looks beautiful."

Troy kissed her cheek. "A flour sack would look beautiful on Cassie."

The line was old and hackneyed, but the way Troy said it made Cassandra's cheeks grow warm. If only she didn't care what he said, but she did.

"There's no comparison between the gown and a flour sack. It's perfect and you know it, Cassandra." Vanessa left no doubt about her opinion. "Do you want me to call Ginger and tell her to order it?"

"I don't know, Mom." Cassandra's gaze lingered on Troy's smile. Those full lips... She would give up ice cream for a year for another taste of him. No matter how hard she tried to forget about his kiss, she couldn't. And it bugged her, immensely. *Remember, only twenty-four more hours to go.* "The dress would be great for spring or summer, but not for a winter wedding."

Vanessa smiled. "Do you have any idea when you'd like to get married?"

"June's a good month," Emily suggested.

Eric nodded his approval. "Very traditional, too. Though you'll have to reserve a place right away. All of the best sites get booked early."

Troy gave Cassandra a soft squeeze. "I've been busy at work so we haven't had time to think about the wedding."

And *we* wouldn't have the time. Come Sunday night, this charade was over. She would wait a couple of weeks, then tell her parents the engagement was off. The reason could be anything from his long hours at work to a fight about where to live to the differences in their life-styles. A perfect plan. As long as she made it through tonight and tomorrow. "Once Troy's job settles down, we'll be able to set a date. We aren't in a rush, are we, honey?" Cassandra emphasized the endearment.

"As long as I know you'll marry me one of these days, pumpkin."

"Honey and pumpkin." Emily grimaced. "How sweet."

Eric looked a little green. "Would you like to go, dear?"

"Be quiet," Emily snapped.

Dixon cleared his throat. "At least we'll have time to prepare a decent prenuptial agreement. I hope this won't be a problem, Troy."

"No problem at all."

"Well, I have a problem with it." Cassandra resisted the urge to stand and put her hands on her hips.

"I knew this was coming," Emily said, not so subtly, to Eric.

Dixon took a sip of brandy. "Cassie, sweetheart, I think a prenuptial agreement is something you should consider."

"Not on your life." Cassandra didn't understand why everything had to revolve around money. She only wanted to be happy. She knew firsthand money couldn't ensure happiness. "It's a marriage, not a business deal."

Dixon finished his snifter of brandy. "Whatever you decide is fine, but at least consider it."

"She will," Troy said, stopping her from saying any more.

"I'm just so excited about your engagement," Dixon admitted. "I only hope we don't have to wait too long for the upcoming nuptials. I can't wait to walk you down the aisle. As I did with your sister."

*Hello.* Who was this man she called father? "Daddy, you're the one who cautioned me about rushing into things. Troy's work schedule is giving us a chance to get to know one another better. It's what you wanted."

"Well, I've changed my mind," Dixon said, surprising Cassandra even more. "I had my doubts at first, but it's obvious you belong together. The twinkle is back in your eyes, sweetheart. I think it has something to do with Troy, and I'm sure you agree with me, too."

Cassandra looked at Vanessa. Her mother made a point of saying young people always rushed into marriage without thinking. She would cite the latest divorce statistics and rest her case. Surely she would support her. "Mother—"

"I agree with your father, Cassandra," Vanessa

said. "No sense having a one- or two-year engagement. Nothing but a waste of time, in my opinion."

Cassandra was running out of supporters. "Emily. What do you think?"

Emily smiled, a charming smile others might call fake and plastic, but Cassandra knew better. Her sister couldn't help being a snob. "Why wait? I think you are one of the cutest couples I've ever seen. In fact, we want to throw an engagement party for you. Isn't that right, Eric?"

His eyes widened. "Yes. We'd, uh, love to throw you an engagement party."

"How does two weeks from tonight sound?" Emily asked.

"Sounds good to me," Dixon said. "This is a wonderful idea. I know several people I'd like Troy to meet."

Vanessa sighed. "Why don't you see what Cassandra and Troy think about it first?"

Caught off guard by the offer, Cassandra didn't know what to say. Part of her was touched. The other part wondered what Emily had up her sleeve. The wary side won out. "That's sweet of you, but I know how busy you both are."

"Think nothing of it, you're my little sister. I've hardly seen you since I got married."

Cassandra wanted to believe the sincerity in her sister's voice, but this was Emily speaking. "I appreciate the offer—"

Emily wasn't listening to her, as usual. "Troy, what do you think? Are you ready to show off your blushing bride-to-be? We were at a gallery opening last night and ran into a couple of your colleagues. None of them knew about your engagement."

Troy tensed. So did Cassandra. She sat stunned, waiting for Emily to drop the bomb about the make-believe engagement.

"My sister might not be the epitome of class and style, but don't tell me you're ashamed of her, Troy."

*Reprieve. No bombshell, yet.*

"Emily," Dixon warned.

*Ignore her comment and say no. Just say no.* Cassandra crossed her fingers.

"Two weeks from tonight sounds great," Troy said.

Damn. So much for her fiancé for the weekend. This gig had been extended. By two weeks. She'd kill him. She'd kill her fiancé, then her sister. No jury would convict her. Not after they heard the evidence.

Emily's smile widened. "Believe me, the pleasure will be all mine. I can't wait to show off my sister and her handsome V.C. fiancé. No one is going to believe it."

"This is going to be so much fun. An engagement party, a bridal shower, a wedding. I can't wait." Vanessa stood. "I'll go get the cake."

Cassandra didn't want a piece of cake, even if it was chocolate. She wanted to show her parents she and Troy did not belong together, that they mustn't have an engagement party thrown in their honor.

The nonstop clink of crystal interrupted her worrying. Emily tapped her glass against Eric's. "Go on and kiss."

"Excuse me?" Cassandra asked, wondering if her sister had finally gone over the deep end.

"When people tap their glasses, you're supposed to kiss," Eric said. "Don't you remember at our wedding? After a few times, you get used to the attention and can enjoy the kisses.''

"That's only at weddings," Troy countered much to Cassandra's delight.

Dixon laughed. "I don't think any of us are going to protest.''

Troy gave her a peck on the cheek.

"You call that a kiss?" Dixon drew his bushy brows together. Emily and Eric continued making the irritating noise.

Troy gave Cassandra a sheepish grin. The devilish gleam in his eyes told her this wasn't going to be a simple peck.

*No way. This wasn't going to happen. This wasn't real.* Cassandra grabbed the edge of the sofa for support.

Troy gave her another kiss—a kiss smack dab on the lips that curled her toes and left her breathless.

How dare he? She clenched her teeth. First the engagement party, now the kiss. She would get even, make him pay.

"Now." Dixon smiled like a proud papa. "Who's ready for some cake?''

# 6

Cassie was angry with him. With three younger sisters, Troy knew the look—narrowed eyes and lips that couldn't decide between tightening and pouting. So he took his time changing into his shorts, brushing his teeth and screwing the cap on the toothpaste. But he couldn't stay in the bathroom all night.

*No sense putting this off any longer.* Opening the door, he took three steps into the room. From out of nowhere, something soft smashed down on his head. "What the—"

Cassie stood next him, armed with a pillow. Her unbraided blond hair fell past her shoulders in waves, reminding him of a lion's mane. She wore his too short, too transparent T-shirt. Underneath he could see the outline of her full breasts and her black panties. "That's for kissing me."

And what a kiss. Thinking about her sweet taste sent his body temperature up, way up. "That wasn't my fault. Blame your father. And Emily and Eric, too."

"How could you kiss me like that?" Eyes gleaming, she stalked him. Troy was so busy looking for peeks of those black panties of hers, he didn't move quickly enough to avoid a feathered blow to his stomach.

"We were supposed to act like the perfect couple. Can I help it if my little peck didn't do the trick? Dixon wanted a real kiss."

"Real kiss, my foot." Turning, she whacked him on the back. "That was for telling Emily she could throw us an engagement party. How could you?"

"How could I say no? She accused me of being ashamed of you. I couldn't back down." He eyed Cassie's pillow warily. "Don't forget, I'm your McKnight in shining armor."

"Do I look like a damsel in distress?" She faked him out and thwacked him in the stomach. "We had an agreement. You're supposed to be my fiancé for the weekend."

"So I'm your fiancé for two more weeks. It's not that bad."

"What do you know about bad?"

"Two weeks, Cassie." Troy tried hard not to stare at her long legs. "Then I'm out of your life forever." He didn't like the sound of forever. Not at all.

"I wanted you out of my life tomorrow."

Liar. He could see it in her eyes. He knew it from the way she responded to his kiss. "You can't always get everything you want, Cassie."

"Wanna bet?" She tried hitting him again, but Troy ducked out of the way, leaving her to swish the air. He grabbed his pillow off the bed. She wanted to play rough, did she?

Two could play at this game. Troy's gaze locked with hers. They stood facing each other, two duelers armed with pillows and a lust for vengeance. He had to smile at the serious expression on her face.

"Are you sure you want to do this? I must warn you—I can hold my own." Troy felt it was only fair to warn her. The oldest of six children, he'd earned his stripes as the pillow-fighting champion of the McKnight clan. "I'm ready to let it drop if you are."

She met his peace offer with a smug smile and a swing of her pillow that hit him solidly on his arm. She had declared war.

"You asked for it." Tightening his grip on the pillow, Troy swung and smacked Cassie on her stomach.

"No fair." She ran to the other side of the room.

Why wasn't it fair? He'd given her a chance, but she'd chosen not to take it. She knew he was bigger than she was. Still the surprised expression on her face told him he'd caught her off guard. "We'll see what's fair." He staged a full-frontal assault.

She swung her pillow back and forth. Like a welterweight boxer trying to fight the heavyweight world champion, she landed few hits. If she knew what was good for her, she would take his advice and give up. But as far as he could tell, Cassie never did what she was told. Nor did she ever admit she was wrong. Dixon had warned him about that.

"Are you ready to give up?" Troy asked.

She smiled, but defiance flickered in her eyes. "No."

Stepping toward her, he raised his eyebrows. "It's your choice."

With a yelp, Cassie flailed wildly with her pillow. He easily blocked her efforts. "Always the gentleman, Troy, aren't you?"

Smiling wickedly, he swung the pillow down on her head. "Of course."

"I'll get you for that."

"I don't think so." Troy laughed. Cassie was like a Chihuahua trying to take on a rottweiler. She didn't stand a chance. As she climbed on her bed, Troy cornered her against the wall. "Do you give up, now?"

She swung her pillow, but he ducked. The pillow swooshed over his head. "No."

His pillow hit her legs, nearly knocking her over. She held her arms out to balance herself. Somehow she managed to stay on her feet. "Now?" he asked.

She crouched lower. Using her pillow as a shield, she peeked over it. "Never."

Troy laughed. He'd give her another reason. "I'm bigger than you."

"I'm smarter than you."

She made a final swing.

Enough was enough. Troy grabbed her pillow in midair and threw it across the room.

Cassie glanced at the pillow lying on the floor. Her mouth gaped open. Narrowing her eyes, she stared at him. "You—"

He aimed his pillow at her and she stopped talking. "Can't think of anything to say, Cassie? If you were one of my brothers or sisters, I'd make you say I was ruler of the universe."

"Well, I'm not going to say it."

No, she wasn't. He wouldn't be that cruel. "You can say I'm the perfect fiancé."

"Perfectly insane fiancé." She attacked him, tickling him.

"Stop it."

"So, I've found a weakness," Cassie said, sounding triumphant. "Give me my pillow."

He backed away, but she followed. "No."

"Then suffer, insane fiancé of mine."

She attacked him, tickling his sides until he couldn't stand it anymore. He tried to pin her arms, but couldn't because she kept squirming away. She continued tickling him. He tickled her back. She wouldn't stop; neither would he. Cassie giggled like a child, her face mere inches from his.

The tickling stopped.

One look into Cassie's eyes was all it took. His heart rate accelerated. The desire to kiss her overwhelmed him.

Her slightly parted lips were the only invitation Troy needed. He lowered his mouth to hers. She opened her mouth further. This wasn't a pretend kiss to please her parents; this one wasn't for show. No one was watching them; no one else cared.

But Troy did.

Feeling as if he would never be able to get enough of her, he savored the taste of her. Warm, wet, sweet. Addictive, her kisses were definitely addictive.

She leaned her head back so he could kiss her neck. ''Oh, Troy.''

So sweet. No expensive perfume could compete against the simplicity of her scent. She smelled like fresh cut flowers on a spring day.

Her T-shirt inched up. Her bare stomach touched his, igniting a fire within him. He ran his hand along her flat belly, her soft skin, until he cupped one of her breasts.

She was perfect.

Cassie moaned. The sound drove him crazy, nearly pushed him over the edge. He wanted her; he'd never wanted anything more in his life. ''Cassie.''

She felt so soft, so right.

She rolled over and straddled him. Leaning over,

she showered kisses from his lips to his chest, then kissed one of his nipples.

His breath caught in his throat. His erection pressed against her belly. "Cassie, we have to stop."

She rubbed her hand along the length of him. "No."

He couldn't take much more. The things she was doing with her mouth, with her hands were driving him crazy. Closing his eyes, he tried imagining an icy winter scene. Instead he pictured a beach on a hot Caribbean day. The beating sun, sweat-drenched skin, the taste of salt.

He couldn't think; he didn't want to think. But he had to for both their sakes. "Stop."

"Do you want to stop?" she whispered, then ran her tongue along the edge of his ear to the lobe.

*Don't stop.* All of the things he'd imagined at the ice-cream parlor, she was doing. "I…" he said, his breathing ragged.

"I don't want to stop." She smiled, accelerating the speed of her hand. "I don't think you want to stop, either."

*Gain control.* But it was so hard. Not only her words, but the seductive tone of her voice told him she wanted to take this all the way. He wanted it, too, but… "This will complicate things."

"I don't—" she paused to nibble on his ear "—care."

Of course she didn't care. Cassie never worried about the consequences. She acted from her heart, for the moment. But he wasn't like that.

He was going to lose it. Troy gritted his teeth. This shouldn't be happening. He was in Dixon Daniels's house; Troy wanted to make love to Dixon's daughter.

No way. It wasn't worth the risk.

Grabbing her hand, Troy pushed it away. To soften the harshness of his gesture, he kissed her gently. "We can't do this."

She glanced at the floor and took a deep breath.

"Cassie." Troy lifted her chin so she had to look at him. He'd done the right thing. She'd told him she wasn't interested in dating. She probably wasn't interested in a fling, either. "I want you, but not like this. Not when we're in the middle of this charade. Do you understand?"

Her lips swollen from his kisses, her eyes wide with desire, she nodded.

"You are an incredibly beautiful and sexy woman." He caressed her smooth cheek. "You know, you're driving me crazy."

"I—"

"Shh." He placed his fingertip on her mouth. Talking about it would only make it worse. He would talk to her in the morning. "Let's get some sleep or at least try to."

Troy was on her bed, but it didn't matter. He wasn't going to sleep tonight. Too many things had happened; too many things hadn't. Holding Cassie would be pure torture, but not holding her would be more painful. "Do you mind if I sleep here tonight?"

Cassie jumped off the bed. "No."

"Where are you going?"

Glancing at the other bed, she bit her lip. Troy wanted to say something to tell her how she made him feel, but couldn't. He couldn't tell her the thought of her sent his hormones into overdrive. He couldn't tell her he wanted to strip off the scrap of black lace she called underwear and make love to her. He couldn't tell her the truth.

"I was hoping you would sleep here, too," Troy said, unable to find any explanation for his need to sleep next to her. Maybe Cassie was right when she called him the perfectly insane fiancé. "Crawl in."

She did. As she lay next to him, her breasts pressed against his chest. Troy held her, trying to keep his hands and his body under control. Slowly the stiffness faded from her body. The gentle, even sound of her breathing told him she must be asleep, but he was afraid to look, afraid of what he might do.

His hands wanted to stray and caress the softness of her moonlit skin. His lips hungered for a taste of her. His body ached for fulfillment, but it wasn't going to happen.

Not tonight.

He would remain in control, even if he had to stay awake all night. Staring at the ceiling, he refused to wish upon another falling star. Look where it had gotten him. Troy released a slow breath. It was going to be another long night. And an even longer two weeks.

The next morning, Cassandra woke to the sound of Troy's heart beating in her ear. His musky male scent teased her nose. The hair on his leg tickled her calf. She snuggled closer, basking in the warmth, the security he provided. He felt so good. Yawning, she let the soothing rhythm of his breathing and heartbeat lull her back to sleep.

She and Troy—a real couple.

What a wonderful dream.

Her eyes sprang open. Sunlight filled the room. This was no dream. Cassandra stared at Troy, a night's growth of whiskers covering his face. His closed eyes and the carefree expression on his face told her he was still asleep.

Troy's chest rose and fell with his even breaths. His normally tousled hair was even more disheveled. He looked like a little boy, but he wasn't. Troy McKnight was a man, one hundred percent male. He'd shown a tenderness last night that touched her and a passion that left her begging for more. Wanting more now.

Oh boy, last night had changed everything and nothing. She sighed. Troy wasn't hers. Wouldn't ever be hers. Yet, it had felt so good, so right.

*But it wasn't real.*

She touched Troy's chest, fingering the light cover of hair. It felt real. More real than her dream the other night. She felt safe and peaceful. Odd feelings considering the disturbing effect Troy had on her senses. Strange, but she felt as though she belonged.

*But it wasn't real.*

Cassandra brushed a stray lock of hair off his forehead. Once again, she imagined a flower-filled church, a tuxedo-clad Troy and her in the beautiful English garden gown. It wasn't difficult to do.

*They weren't really engaged.*

But that was a technicality.

*Or was it?*

Her mind countered every reason her heart brought forward. Suddenly a new awareness hit her. Cassandra swallowed the lump lodged in her throat. She was falling for Troy McKnight. Falling hard.

That was the only explanation for her actions. But falling for him, wanting to make love with him made no sense. She didn't want to feel that way. She didn't want to fall in love. Not with Troy, not with any man.

Even if, and that was a big if, she did want to fall in love, Troy was everything she didn't want in a man—a venture capitalist, materialistic, ambitious, predictable. A man exactly like her ex-fiancé. As she had once been.

So what if Troy was also intelligent, caring, gorgeous, polite? She knew better than to follow her heart. Experience had taught her that. She should have been more careful. What a fool. She'd set herself up for a big letdown, that's what she'd done.

Troy opened his eyes. The dark circles under them told her he was tired, but he smiled when he saw her. "Good morning."

Her stomach tingled. *Tingles meant nothing, absolutely nothing.* "Good morning."

"Did you sleep well?"

"I, uh," Cassandra faltered, unable to find the right words. Troy's smile turned her on. She wanted to touch him, to kiss him, to make love to him. But she didn't want to make another mistake. In two weeks he would be out of her life forever. Taking this any further would be a big mistake. He was rigid; he had a life plan. It wouldn't work.

He tensed. "Is something wrong, Cassie?"

"Of course not." She pulled the comforter up to her neck. Cassandra wasn't modest, but Troy made her feel shy. The thin fabric of her T-shirt and her panties provided scant protection from his assessing gaze.

It would be so easy to keep pretending he was really hers. Her parents looked happy; she felt happy. But if she continued it a little longer, she would get hurt. She'd been that route before and swore never again. But Troy...she remembered how her body responded to his kiss, his touch. She'd never felt that way before. Certainly not with Eric.

"Are you having regrets?"

Cassandra wished she had regrets, but she didn't. Troy made her feel alive, beautiful and special. "No."

"So what's wrong?"

"Last night was…well, it was wonderful."

Smiling, he kissed her hand. "Wonderful. I wish we could have gone further. I'm sorry we had to stop."

He wasn't making this any easier. How could she tell him she didn't want to get hurt without making herself vulnerable? She pulled her hand away. "I know, but—"

His eyes darkened to the color of a stormy sea. "But, what?"

This wasn't going to be easy. Not with her heart wanting one thing and her mind another. She knew what to do, the only thing to do. "I started thinking about the, uh, complications of our actions."

"And?"

*I'm falling in love with you. I can't let that happen.* "We have nothing in common, but there is some kind of—"

"Chemistry," he said.

*Understatement of the year.* "Yes, but you were right to stop."

Silent, his eyebrows furrowed. "I'm glad you agree."

"I do," Cassandra said, wishing for once Troy hadn't agreed with her.

Cassandra rinsed off the last of the breakfast plates and placed it in the dishwasher. She gazed out the kitchen window. A slight breeze rippled the clear water in the pool. Her family and Troy sat on the patio outside. Five people drinking coffee on a Sunday morning under a sunny, blue sky. Five people who shared outlooks and goals. Five people who she didn't want to be like.

She poured powdered detergent into the soap tray, wondering how the situation had gotten so out of control. In one weekend Troy had managed to do two things—fit in with her family and worm his way into her heart. He'd helped her handle her meddling parents and she appreciated that, but she hadn't expected to go away from the weekend caring about him. She wanted to forget about his kisses, his warmth. She wanted to forget about Troy McKnight. Except it wasn't going to be easy with their engagement party in two weeks.

Damn. Cassandra slammed the dishwasher door and locked it.

Troy tapped on the window. "Are you almost done, Cassie?" he asked through the screen.

She didn't want to go outside. She felt safer, more comfortable inside. The more time she spent with Troy, the more she wanted to spend with him. A lose-lose situation. "I'll be out in a minute."

He glanced back at her family. "You'd better hurry."

Troy wore a white T-shirt under a blue chambray shirt and a pair of khaki shorts. He looked as though he'd stepped off the pages of a Gap ad. Her mouth went dry. "What's wrong?"

"Your family is getting carried away."

"I told you—"

"It's more than that. You won't believe who Dixon wants to invite to the engagement party."

Maybe a puppy would make her feel all warm and fuzzy the way Troy did. Or a kitten. Cats were easier to deal with than dogs. And she could take a cat to the bookstore. "Who?"

He rambled off a list of names, including several of the power brokers in Silicon Valley. It was an up-and-coming V.C.'s perfect guest list. Troy would be in heaven; she would be in hell. "That's quite a list."

He shrugged.

A shrug? "Aren't you excited?"

His forehead wrinkled. "What if something goes wrong? I've worked so hard and am so close…. This could turn into a complete disaster."

It already was a disaster, but she wasn't going to tell him that. "Nothing will go wrong. I will be the perfect fiancée and you will impress them so much they'll all wonder why you aren't working for them."

"Thanks. I needed to hear that." He seemed to breathe a sigh of relief. "But you should get out here. Emily and your mother are deciding where we should register."

"Register?"

"For wedding presents."

His smile sent her pulse racing. Cassandra wiped off the counter. "That isn't funny."

"I'm not joking."

"But we aren't engaged." She lowered her voice. "We can't accept presents."

"We'll return them after you break my heart."

Very funny, McKnight. He'd exit the relationship without a scratch. "How come you get to be the one with the broken heart?"

He glanced down.

"That's right." She washed her hands. "You don't want to offend the mighty Dixon Daniels."

"It's not that."

"Yes, it is." Remembering Troy's main concern was his career put things back into perspective for her. Just like Eric. He and Eric could be twins. She dried her hands on a dish towel.

"Please, come outside." Troy shoved one of his hands into his shorts' pocket and jiggled some change. "I need you."

*If only you did need me....* She turned on the dishwasher. "I'm coming."

How hard could this be? A little chitchat, then she could go home. Home to an empty apartment and no messages on her answering machine. Maybe she did need a pet.

Carrying the coffeepot, Cassandra walked outside. "Anyone need a refill?"

Dixon took the pot from her and set it on the glass-top table. "Have a seat, Cassie."

Troy patted the pillow on the empty wrought-iron chair next to him. "Come here, sweetie pie."

Vanessa smiled. "Cassandra, we've been discussing the engagement party. You need to register for wedding presents."

"That isn't necessary, Mom."

"But it is," Vanessa said. "I know the perfect place. I'll make an appointment for you this week."

"I have to work."

"I know, sweetheart, but you have employees who work for you. I'll make an evening appointment and go with you. We'll have so much fun like we did shopping for your wedding dress."

Cassandra wanted her parents out of her life, not driving up midweek to help her pick out china and crystal patterns. Think positive, she told herself. Two more weeks and it would be over. No more interference, matchmaking or wedding plans. Two weeks wasn't that long. Wars had been lost in less time. "Sure."

"About the engagement party." Emily tossed her shiny black hair behind her shoulder. "We've decided a black-tie affair might be too much, considering the short notice."

"Of course, black-tie optional won't work, either," Eric added. His words earned him a smile from his wife.

"You are right, as usual, Eric." Emily patted his hand like a woman petting her trained lap dog.

Cassandra wondered why she ever thought she was in love with Eric Wainwright. Marrying him would have been a disaster. Being with Troy made her realize how wrong Eric was for her. She also saw how right Eric was for her sister. Emily could be as bossy and demanding as she wanted and Eric wouldn't complain. He would ask how high she wanted him to jump. The two were a perfect match.

"We wouldn't mind if you moved the date." Troy entwined his warm fingers with Cassandra's. Her stomach fluttered. She tried pulling her hand away, but he wouldn't let go.

"I wouldn't dream of doing that." Emily pursed her lips. "Let's make it semiformal dress. We can go shopping next week. I know all of the best boutiques in the city. We'll go every day until we find something…spectacular."

Cassandra appreciated the offer, but wasn't ready

for spending that much time with Emily. Lunch would
be a good start, not shopping every day. And Cassandra couldn't help but wonder if Emily meant finding
her something suitable, rather than spectacular, to
wear.

"That's nice of you to offer," Troy said. "But I've
been wanting to buy Cassie a new outfit and this will
give me the perfect opportunity to buy her something
special."

Unbelievable. This couldn't be happening. But it
was.

Cassandra stared at Troy, at everyone. She'd invented her fiancé to stop her parents' meddling. But
it wasn't working. She not only had her parents involved with making engagement and wedding plans,
but her sister and brother-in-law, too.

And Troy. Didn't he realize he wasn't helping?
Enough was enough.

"I have an idea that will solve all of our problems,"
Cassandra said. "Why not make the party clothing
optional?"

# 7

"Clothing optional?" Troy focused on the road ahead. "Don't you think that was a bit extreme?"

"Extreme is the only thing that works with my family."

"I thought your mother and Emily were going to faint."

"They aren't the fainting types," Cassie said. "Besides I had to do something. My mother was so fired up about registering. She would have our wedding invitations picked out, addressed and in the mail if we hadn't left when we did."

Tension filled the cab of his pickup. Troy didn't need an antenna to pick up a radio station, not with Cassie sitting so stiffly next to him. He hit the scanner on his radio, until he found a blues station playing the jazzy strains of a saxophone solo.

"This has turned into a huge mess, Troy. I don't want to register for wedding presents."

"I'll come with you." He didn't want to go, but he couldn't leave Cassie to deal with it on her own. They were in this together. "When are you going?"

"Wednesday night. But I don't want you to come. It'll be easier without you."

"Then I won't go," he said, relieved. "But the

party... Cassie, it could be a real boost to my career. An introduction to the V.C. inner circle. I know you're not interested in the party."

"Interested?" She chuckled. "It'll be as much fun as the Bhutan Death March. Do you know why Emily is throwing this engagement party?"

"To be nice?"

"She's setting us up for something, but I don't know what. I think she wants us to break up."

*Let Emily try.* "Did she tell you that?"

"No, but it's pretty obvious. Her remark to you and her comment about finding me a dress. I think she's trying to tell you I would be an unsuitable wife."

"You're not unsuitable." He thought about his words. He couldn't afford to forget Cassie wasn't his type. "You'll make someone a great wife."

"Someone is the key word. Someone who isn't a rising star in the venture capital arena."

True. Cassie rejected the very world he was struggling so hard to make a life in. It wouldn't work. Unless she just needed the right encouragement to change her mind. "Do you hate the business that much?"

"Yes. And our engagement party will be the epitome of all that is wrong with it."

Had Eric taken her to parties or perhaps Dixon? Troy tried to picture her among the caviar and free-flowing wine and champagne, but couldn't. She didn't fit in with the social-climbing crowd. She would be out of place and have little in common with the trophy spouses and dates. "Have you attended enough parties to know for sure?"

"I used to work for Richardson and Scott."

Richardson and Scott was one of the largest and

most prestigious investment banking firms in the country. Cassie with her flowing skirts and oversize shirts and sweaters worked at the traditional firm? He couldn't picture it. "What did you do?"

"I was a research analyst." By the tone of her voice, he would have thought she was a member of a firing squad. "Computer software, and I also did a stint in M & A."

His spontaneous, rule-breaking, tattooed Cassie had been a research analyst and worked in mergers and acquisitions? Troy wondered if she had an M.B.A. "Why aren't you still there?"

"I didn't like it."

"But it's a great company. Long hours, but the compensation makes up for it."

He caught her shrug from the corner of his eye. "I still didn't like it."

What didn't she like? Richardson and Scott had a solid mentor program and promoted more women than any of the other big firms. She must have been out of her mind to quit...or been fired. "Why?"

"Lots of reasons. I hated getting up early. I hated working late, especially during reporting season. I hated all of the office politics." Cassie grimaced. "But most of all I hated wearing panty hose every day."

Panty hose? She gave up a tremendous career because of panty hose? With her long, shapely legs, she'd be a knockout in panty hose and heels. Troy would have stared at her in disbelief, but he didn't want to look away from the road. "You were burned-out. Why didn't you take a leave of absence?"

"I did." She smiled. "I took a permanent leave of absence."

"But—"

"You don't get it, do you?" Cassie bit her lip. "It wasn't just the job, Troy. I hated the entire investment industry. It made me miserable. I never smiled. I was on the verge of getting an ulcer. It was awful. I would stare at the mirror and not recognize myself. My priorities got screwed up, and I lost sight of who I was inside."

"But you must have had everything."

"Oh, I had a great flat in the Marina, designer clothes and a German-built convertible. I was making lots of money, but when you're working eighty hours a week and unhappy, what good is it? It didn't take long to realize money wasn't as important as I thought it was."

But money was important. If Cassie had grown up as he had, struggling to make ends meet every month, every day, she'd think differently. "That's easy to do when you have your father to fall back on."

"I have never fallen back on my father." Anger flared in her eyes. "Do you think my daddy sends me a check every month?"

"I don't know what to think."

"I own a bookstore. I used the money I saved when I worked for Richardson and Scott, sold my car and borrowed the rest." Cassie wrinkled her nose. "At least those long hours got me something worthwhile."

Her words surprised Troy. She didn't seem the type to devote the time needed to make a business successful. "What about the gas money?"

"All of the money my father gives me I save. Once a year I use it to buy him gift certificates for rounds of golf at his favorite courses in the Bay Area. Has your curiosity been appeased?"

"Yes." Troy had upset her. "I shouldn't have assumed—"

"Can I ask you a question?"

"Yes."

"Why is money so important to you?"

He hesitated. "You wouldn't understand."

"Try me."

"You grew up with the proverbial silver spoon. I grew up on a farm where my parents struggled to put food on the table, to dress us in clothes that fit." Troy sighed. "We never had any money. Never."

He continued. "One Christmas we had a really rough time. Rain had damaged the crops that fall. My father had broken his leg. There wasn't enough money for presents. My mother and I stayed up all night on Christmas Eve. We baked cookies and made candies so my brothers and sisters would have something in their stockings on Christmas morning." Troy gripped the steering wheel, remembering how haggard his mother had looked. "That Christmas, I decided I would never struggle like my parents. I wanted to be able to provide for my family, put food on the table and presents under the Christmas tree."

"How old were you?" Cassie asked.

"Twelve."

"Were you happy?"

"Yes, before I realized how much my parents struggled," he said. "I know it's hard for you to understand, Cassie. But please don't romanticize it. Being poor and happy don't go hand in hand."

She stared out the window. "Neither does being rich and happy."

Tuesday night, Troy hung up the telephone. Leave it to Vanessa Daniels. The woman wouldn't take no for an answer. Damn. Cassie was not going to be happy. He'd better tell her the news so she had time to cool down. A pillow fight was one thing, but he couldn't afford to have her smashing china and crystal at one of the most exclusive stores in San Francisco.

Not that he didn't want to talk to Cassie. He did. He wanted to see her, too. Being with her drove him crazy; being away from her drove him crazy. He couldn't win. Troy picked up the telephone and dialed her number.

After four rings, her answering machine picked up. ''Hi, you've reached Cassandra's answering machine. At the beep, you know what to do…''

Before he could hang up, the machine beeped. ''Hi, Cassie. This is Troy, Troy McKnight. Your mother called and invited me to go register with you. Before I knew what was happening, I got roped in. Give me a call.''

Damn, he hated answering machines. Troy hung up the phone. He brushed his hand through his hair, hoping he didn't sound as stupid as he thought he sounded. And her message…

Why did she say her name?

She should say only her telephone number and *we* cannot get to the phone right now. Didn't she know anything about living in a big city? She needed to protect herself and take precautions.

Troy glanced at his digital alarm clock. Nine o'clock. He didn't know what time her bookstore closed, but she must still be at work. She would call him when she got home.

At eleven o'clock, Troy got worried. Surely her bookstore didn't stay open late. If she wasn't at the bookstore, where was she? More importantly, who was with her?

Staring at the phone, he willed it to ring. It didn't. He drummed his fingers on the desk. His fingers picked up pace until all he could hear was the *rat-tat-tatting* rhythm of "From the Shores of Montezuma." When he finished the song he started again. He didn't want to stop, because without the noise, he'd be sitting in his silent bedroom thinking about calling her again.

By midnight, Troy paced his apartment. He couldn't sleep; he couldn't work. She still hadn't called. He picked up the telephone and called her. When her machine answered, Troy slammed the receiver down.

What if something happened to her? An accident or… His gut tightened. Waiting was hell. But it could be worse. A lot worse. Imagine what he'd be going through if she were his real fiancée…

As Cassandra entered her apartment, she yawned. It had been a long night. She hadn't meant to work so late, but she hadn't realized how much work needed to be done. Work that couldn't be done with a store crowded with customers. Work that kept her from sitting at home and daydreaming about Troy.

She dropped her backpack on the floor and unlaced her black boots. A sharp pain shot up her back when she bent over. That's what she got for sleeping on the hard floor last night. Oh, well, a hot shower would help. She kicked off her boots.

She caught a glimpse of the blinking red light on her answering machine. Her only thought was of sleep, but the message could be important. Too tired to lift her feet, she shuffled her way across the hardwood floor. Dust from her unswept floor clung to her socks.

She pressed the button and the tape rewound.

"You have two messages," the digital unisex voice said. "Message delivered Tuesday, 8:14 p.m."

"Hi, Cassandra," Vanessa said. "Sorry to bother you, but I had the most wonderful idea. What if we bring Troy with us tomorrow? Wouldn't that be fun? I'll call him since you're gone. Maybe I'll find you at Troy's. Otherwise, I'll see you tomorrow night at the store. Seven o'clock. Don't be late."

Great. Just what she needed, her mother watching her and Troy select a china pattern. Cassandra hoped he had nixed the idea, but she was too tired to think about it. She didn't want to think about the engagement party or registering for wedding presents or her soon-to-be ex-fiancé. She wanted to sleep.

"Message delivered Tuesday, 8:59 p.m," the machine's voice said.

Cassandra rubbed her tired eyes. The machine beeped. "Hi, Cassie. This is Troy, Troy McKnight. Your mother called and invited me to go register with you. Before I knew what was happening, I got roped in. Give me a call."

"End of messages," the electronic voice said.

Cassandra thought for a moment, trying to ignore her sleepiness. Roped in? Troy was too polite. He probably said yes without a fight.

What time was it? She pressed the clock button on her answering machine. "It is Wednesday, 8:07 a.m."

So early. No wonder she couldn't keep her eyes open. She should be asleep. She had to be back at the store at noon so she could take off early tonight. And pick out china and crystal and...

And this sucked.

Cassandra stretched, lifting her arms toward the ceiling. Oh, boy, her back hurt. She needed to buy a futon for the back room of the bookstore. No more sleeping on the floor.

She stared at the telephone. She should call Troy and tell him not to come, but she didn't want to talk to him. Okay, maybe a little. If only she could forget about him, but that was easier said than done. Troy McKnight was a hard man to forget.

Eight o'clock. Troy would be on his way to work, so she wouldn't have to talk to him. She could leave a message on his answering machine. Perfect.

Cassandra dug through the scraps of paper piled near her phone until she found his business card. Troy had scribbled his home number on the back. She dialed the number.

On the third ring, the machine picked up. "Hello."

Cassandra waited for the rest of the message, but heard a second hello instead. She panicked for a second. Only psycho ex-girlfriends or ex-wives called men and hung up on them. Common sense told her to say hello, so she did. "Hi, Troy."

"Cassandra?"

"Yes," she said, thinking he should be at work. Not that she cared. All she cared about was why hearing him say her name made her feel all warm and tingling. "I was happy to hear your message."

"You were?" He sounded surprised.

Damn. Happy wasn't the right word. Boy, what a scatterbrain she was when she didn't get enough sleep. "Actually I meant I got your message."

"Isn't it a little early for you to be up?"

"I just got home."

"You just got home?"

"Uh-huh." She yawned. "Aren't you going to work today?"

"I have a breakfast meeting."

"That sounds like fun." Like a trip to the dentist, she added silently. She leaned her head back. Another pain shot up her back. "Ow."

"Are you okay, Cassie?"

"I'm tired and my back is killing me." She yawned again, thinking how nice it would feel to crawl into her comfortable, warm bed. It would be nicer if Troy was with her. Too dangerous to think like that. She must really be tired. "I didn't get much sleep last night. I'm going to bed as soon as I hang up the phone."

Static sounded. "Troy?"

More silence.

Had they been disconnected? "Are you there?"

"I'm here," he said finally.

Cassandra shrugged, sending another knife-edged pain shooting through her back. She didn't know what his problem was, nor did she care right now. "You don't have to come tonight."

Cassandra pictured herself and Troy selecting dishes and appliances and bedding. Very couplelike, very intimate. The line between fact and fiction was blurring. This wouldn't do much to help. "Don't you think it will be, uh, awkward?"

"Yes, but your mother thought I should come."

"You're turning into the dutiful son-in-law."

"I don't have a choice."

No, Troy didn't. He wasn't coming to please her. Ambition was a powerful motivator. "I know."

"I'll pick you up and drive you to Union Square,"

he said. "Your bookstore's on Twenty-fourth Street in Noe Valley, right?"

Cassandra yawned. "Yes."

"What's the name?"

Her heavy eyelids drooped so she forced them open. "Cassandra's Attic."

"I'll come by at six-thirty."

"Okay." She stifled another yawn. She didn't want to think about seeing Troy. All she wanted to think about was a couple of hours of uninterrupted, comfortable sleep. "And, Troy, thanks. I know this isn't easy for you, either."

"No problem."

Black spots appeared before her eyes and the room blurred. She had to get some sleep. "I'll see you tonight."

That evening, Troy walked along Twenty-fourth Street. The smell of olive oil and lamb wafted in the air as he passed a crowded Greek restaurant. He inhaled, wondering if the food tasted as good as it smelled. His stomach growled. He hadn't eaten much at breakfast or lunch. He couldn't eat. Thanks to Cassie.

She must have met someone else. But she told him she wasn't interested in dating. Whoever it was must be someone special.

Hell, she was already sleeping with him. She'd even hurt her back doing it. Didn't Saturday night mean anything to her? It wasn't a simple, meaningless kiss. It was more.

Warning bells sounded.

Danger signs illuminated.

He was falling for Cassie Daniels. And falling in a way he hadn't done before.

It didn't make sense. His once routine life was being taken over by a woman who would think nothing of ordering dessert first at a five-star restaurant. A woman who would jump out of an airplane then check to see if she were wearing a parachute. A woman he'd known a little more than a week. Troy's stomach knotted.

*Dammit.*

He didn't want to feel this way. He had a great job with a partnership on the horizon. In a few years, he'd be a millionaire and have everything he ever wanted. He'd never have to worry about taking care of his family, about anything. He didn't need this. So why was he so bothered?

Because he couldn't stop thinking about Cassie kissing another man. Troy wanted to punch someone, preferably her new guy. As his temperature rose, he shoved his fists into his pockets.

It took him a minute to realize he had walked past the bookstore. He retraced his steps. Standing in front of the window, he peered in. Cassandra's Attic was larger than he thought it would be. Besides the main floor, there was a loft—most likely ''the attic.'' He'd expected her store to specialize in New Age books. He didn't know why, but the display of *New York Times* Bestsellers in the window surprised him.

Cassie stood behind the counter. Smiling, she talked to a customer. She wore a ponytail, but a few blond tendrils had fallen, framing her face. Pale pink crystals dangled from her ears and matched her T-shirt. She also wore a lace vest. She was beautiful.

And she was involved with someone else.

Troy exhaled slowly, wondering what to do next. He couldn't stand here all night.

Walking into the store, he caught the scent of cinnamon and cloves in the air. The wooden shelves were battered and scratched, but they fit the casual atmosphere. The walls could use a new coat of paint. The shelves, if arranged differently, would make better use of the space. She could convert the upstairs to a coffee bar. But even without the improvements, the store had a small town charm, something he hadn't felt in a long time.

Glancing around, he noticed her customers felt the same way. A man with jet black hair sat on a wooden chair, thumbing through a large book about lighthouses. Toward the back of the store, a woman read to her two children. Several others lounged on stools reading books and magazines.

"I'll be with you in a minute, Troy," Cassie said from behind the counter. She turned her attention to an elderly woman. Cassie dashed out from behind the counter and hurried down an aisle. She pulled a paperback from one of the shelves and rushed back. As she rang up the sale, she laughed with the woman as if she were an old friend. As soon as Cassie finished with her, another customer stepped up to the counter, a stack of paperbacks in her hands.

Cassie glanced at Troy.

"Go ahead," he said. "I'm early."

Watching this responsible, business side of Cassie intrigued Troy. He had recognized her intelligence, but she seemed too free-spirited to run a successful business on her own. But from what he could see, she was doing fine. Not an easy task for an independent bookseller. Troy smiled. He liked this side of Cassie, a side earning his respect.

As another customer walked up to the counter, Cassie yelled, "Moe."

A young man raced down the stairs. He had short black hair with what resembled a six-inch Mohawk down the center. He was tall and thin with an ear-to-ear grin. Cassie whispered something into the man's ear, and Moe stepped behind the counter.

As Cassie walked toward Troy, she swung her small purse over her shoulder. Her long, black skirt flowed around her legs. "I'm sorry you had to wait."

"You have a nice bookstore."

She smiled. "Thanks."

Troy motioned to the man behind the counter, who watched every move Cassie made. "Does he work for you?"

She glanced back. "You mean Moe?"

Troy nodded.

"I don't know what I'd do without him. He's my right hand."

Was Moe her new boyfriend? Troy gritted his teeth. He wondered where this Moe person came from and why he was working at the bookstore. "How long has he worked for you?"

"Since I opened. I have no idea where he came from, but he's been my guardian angel since he walked into the place." She faced Moe. "Bye."

Moe smiled, a lop-sided grin Troy thought looked fake. But most women would be fooled by it. He should warn Cassie. "Have fun, Cass."

Cass. Moe called her Cass? Troy waited for her to correct Moe. She merely smiled. "Are you ready, Troy?"

Ready to kill Moe. Was he the one who hurt her back? Troy clenched his fist. "Does Moe stand for Mohawk?"

Cassie laughed. "Of course, not. It's a nickname. His real name is Zack."

Troy didn't know why he was torturing himself, but he had to ask. "Why Moe?"

"He's a big Three Stooges fan. He didn't think Curly fit him. His brother is named Larry and who wants to be called Shemp?" she said matter-of-factly, reminding him of when she'd asked him to be her fiancé. Look where that had got him.

*Okay, time to go.* Troy opened the door for her. "By the way, are you feeling better?"

Why did he ask her that? He didn't want to know the details. Troy never realized he was a masochist.

"I am, thank you." Cassandra walked outside the store. "It's my own fault you know. Moe told me, but I wouldn't listen."

Troy did not want to hear the intimate details of her night of passion with a man named after one of the Three Stooges. "Cassie, I—"

"He told me I wasn't twenty anymore, that I couldn't stay up all night and work on—"

"Cassie, I really—" Troy paused. What did she say? "Work?"

"Yes," she said. "I was trying to stack books and figure out how to rearrange the shelves. Moe had to leave around two o'clock. He made me promise I wouldn't walk home alone."

Way to go, Moe. Someone needed to look out for Cassie. Troy wanted to shake the man's hand. "What about your back?"

"I slept on the floor in the storeroom. Guess I'm not a young pup anymore."

"None of us is anymore," Troy said, feeling enormously relieved. No need to be jealous. Not that he ever was, he convinced himself. Jealous? Him? No way.

# 8

As Cassandra rode the escalator to the third floor, she stared at Troy's reflection in the mirror to her left. He looked like a successful venture capitalist in his charcoal gray double-breasted suit. Who was she kidding? He looked gorgeous, period.

Not her type?

What a joke.

Even his desire to be rich didn't cause her attraction to wane. Especially after he'd explained about growing up without money, without presents under the Christmas tree.

She shouldn't have come.

Troy McKnight had haunted her thoughts and her dreams. His first kiss that morning in the breakfast nook reminded her of coffee so much she'd started drinking herbal tea instead. She wet her dry lips.

Now he stood so close to her, only one step down. She resisted the urge to lean back and rest against him.

Hopeless, utterly hopeless. She looked away, fighting another headache thinking about Troy always caused. Resisting the impulse to massage her temples, she clutched the black handrail. The pain drifted away. Too bad Troy couldn't disappear as easily. But he was here. And wasn't going anywhere until after their engagement party.

She stepped from the escalator. Moving forward would put her in the china department, staying put would put her in Troy's arms. Unsure which was worse, Cassandra moved to the side.

Troy took hold of her hand and kissed it.

The fluttery sensations spreading through her meant nothing. "Always the perfect fiancé, aren't you?"

"I try."

He tried too hard. Her hand fit snugly in his, too snugly for her own good. "You can let go. I don't see my mother."

Troy didn't let go of her hand. "She still might be here."

"What time is it?"

"Seven o'clock on the nose."

"My mother should be here. She's always on time." A discreet Bridal Registry sign sat on a cherry, Queen Anne writing desk. Pachelbel's "Canon in D" played on speakers hidden in the ceiling. The place, elegant and refined, reeked of money and society. "Maybe we should check in."

A tall, model-thin woman met them halfway. She wore a stylish lime pantsuit that belonged in the pages of *Vogue*. "My name is Mercedes. May I help you?"

"Hi. I'm Cassandra Daniels." She forced a smile. "This is Troy McKnight, my, uh…"

"Her fiancé." Troy shook Mercedes's hand. "We have an appointment."

"Oh, Ms. Daniels and Mr. McKnight." Mercedes smiled, her pearly white teeth a stark contrast to her dark complexion. "I've been expecting you. Please have a seat."

"My mother is meeting us here."

"Oh, I'm so sorry." Mercedes waved her hand and her jasmine perfume scented the air. "Your mother called to say she won't be able to make the appointment. But don't worry. We'll find the perfect items to fit your life-style."

"Thank you, but we should reschedule." Cassandra tried to sound disappointed.

"Why don't we get started tonight? You can talk to your mother before we finalize anything." Mercedes sat behind the desk. "I can fax a copy of what you select to your mother."

*And give her a full report, too.* Cassandra sighed.

Mercedes took out a file folder and a Mont Blanc pen from the desk. "Let's get started."

Following a ten-minute orientation, Cassandra picked up a clear clipboard and stared at the tasteful displays of crystal, china and hollowware. She couldn't believe she was doing this. They weren't engaged. But she didn't have much of a choice. Not with Mercedes, the spy, watching.

Mercedes motioned them to follow her. "Why don't we start with a china pattern?"

Cassandra brushed a stray lock off his forehead. "Is that all right with you, muffin?"

"I go where you go, shortcake." He drew her close to whisper in her ear. "Why are you being so—so fiancéelike?"

"I think Mercedes is going to report back to my mother," Cassandra whispered back. "Think you can handle it?"

"I'll try."

As he kissed her neck, her pulse hit Mach 1. Maybe she should have worded her question differently. Could she handle it?

"The china is over here, my two lovebirds," Mercedes said.

On the way, Troy pointed out an ivory plate with a black and navy patterned band and a gold rim. "What do you think of this, cupcake?"

"It's beautiful."

"Like you."

The words flowed too easily from his lips. Cassandra could almost believed he meant them. But he didn't. Too bad. "Don't you think it's a little bold? We might grow tired of it, tiger."

"You're absolutely right, kitten."

She picked up a plate with peach and blue flowers along the rim and in the center. "What about this?"

"It's nice." Troy kissed her cheek and Cassandra nearly dropped the expensive plate. "But the colors might not match our decorating scheme in a couple of years. Something neutral might work better."

Cassandra set the plate down. "You're so right, dumpling."

Mercedes beamed. "The two of you are so adorable. I've seen so many couples who are only interested in picking out the most expensive or popular patterns. It's obvious the two of you are more interested in building a home that will last."

Cassandra clasped her hand in Troy's and gazed into his eyes. She wondered if she were doing this for Mercedes's sake or her own. Truth be known, Cassandra didn't care whether Mercedes was a spy or not. "I'm lucky."

Troy caressed her hand with his thumb. "We're lucky."

Standing among the exquisite china and crystal, Cassandra could almost believe they were the happy engaged couple they pretended to be. And she liked the feeling. The strains of Bach played—a tune she could imagine being played as she walked down the aisle.

"Troy's correct about picking a pattern," Mercedes added. "You need a pattern with colors that you love and can grow old with. Don't forget, you will have this china forever."

Troy released her hand and examined another china pattern. His touch warmed her skin. Cassandra wished he was still holding her hand.

As she looked at the different place settings, she pictured her and Troy at Christmas. A great, big Douglas fir and lots of brightly wrapped presents. Joy and laughter. A table overloaded with food and surrounded with family. Children. Traditions that would carry over. And each year, Cassandra would set the table with the same china. A classic pattern. White or ivory. Something...

Wait a minute. Stop the madness. This wasn't for real. They would never have a decorating scheme. No traditions or children. They weren't planning for the future. This was all a lie. *Agree to whatever he picks up next.* Her heart pounded in her throat.

Troy showed her a white plate with raised white strawberries and vines circling the edge. "What about this?"

"Perfect." And it was—to her dismay. If she were going to get married, she would have selected that pattern. But she wasn't getting married. Forget about it. Cassandra readied her pencil. "Eight place settings."

"Twelve." Troy gave her arm a gentle squeeze. "I have a large family. We'll never be able to use them at Thanksgiving and Christmas unless we have enough place settings for everyone. I can almost taste the turkey and homemade cranberry sauce."

So could she, but wait a minute. Thanksgiving and Christmas dinners? She didn't know how to cook a turkey and cranberry sauce came in a can or from the caterer. This was getting ridiculous. "But—"

"Twelve."

"Okay, twelve place settings." It wasn't worth arguing about. Whatever gifts they got would be returned anyway.

"Is this for your formal place setting?" Mercedes asked.

"Yes." Troy ran his fingertips along the edge of the plate.

"We don't need informal dishes," Cassandra added, trying to erase the image of shiny, silver chargers beneath the plates and a Battenburg lace tablecloth. She had left that life behind; she wasn't going back to it. Not for Troy, not for anyone.

Troy smiled. "I want to use our china every day. No sense keeping it locked in a hutch only for holidays. That way, it'll remind us of tonight and how we chose it together."

*I love you, Troy.* Cassandra realized she wasn't falling in love with Troy. She'd fallen. Headfirst.

Mercedes's smile grew wider. "Mr. McKnight, I wish I could clone you."

*I wish you were really mine.* Cassandra's chest tightened. She searched for the nearest exit, but didn't get past staring into Troy's eyes.

*Focus on registering. Forget about him.*

Mercedes set the five-piece place setting on a forest green place mat. "Let's find crystal and silverware to complete the setting."

"What about this?" Troy held a plain goblet with a narrow stem. "I like this one."

"Orrefors," Mercedes said. "Would you care to look at the Waterford patterns also?"

Cassandra remembered Vanessa's comment at the bridal salon. "I'm not the Waterford type. The crystal Troy has picked out is fine."

Troy raised the glass as if making a toast. "If I clink the glass do I get a kiss?"

*You can have anything you want.* Cassandra swallowed hard. "Do you deserve one?"

He tapped his finger on the glass. "Yes."

She only meant to brush against his lips, but the moment hers touched his she couldn't stop herself from really kissing him. Everything faded away. Everything except Troy. The taste of him, the texture of him. She never wanted this moment to end.

*But it wasn't real.*

As she pulled away from Troy, he smiled. "If I always get kisses like that, I should buy one of these glasses tonight. I could get used to that."

So could she. But Cassandra couldn't afford to. Remember the hurt, the betrayal. Her heart was off limits.

"Would you like to see the silverware?" Mercedes asked.

"Yes." Troy held Cassandra's hand once again.

He'd touched her, kissed her, stared at her. She needed to get away from him. Now. Cassandra made a beeline to a display of silverware against the far wall. As soon as they picked the silverware, she could go home. Alone.

Troy followed her. "Look at this, honey."

"It's perfect," she said, wanting to end this charade right now. She had so much on her mind, so much to figure out.

He stared at a dinner fork. "Perfect?"

Cassandra looked at it. The silver fork resembled something from a fantasy novel with dragons on the handle and swirling arrows of gold forming the prongs. "Maybe not."

Mercedes pointed to a setting shining against the black velvet background. "What do you think of this?"

Two circular bands near the head of the fork were the only decoration. Plain, yet striking. Cassandra liked it. And once she selected the flatware she could go home. "Yes, that will do."

Mercedes put the silverware together with the rest of their choices. "Wonderful selections. Look how well the pieces work together."

Troy placed his arm around Cassandra's shoulder. "Doesn't it look perfect, darling?"

*You're perfect.* Cassandra's stomach knotted. "Yes."

Mercedes smiled. "I've seen hundreds of engaged

couples and must say the two of you are a perfect match. You will have a wonderful, happy marriage.''

Cassandra couldn't talk; she couldn't breathe.

Troy pulled her closer. He smelled so good, so mouthwatering good. It wasn't fair. ''Thank you, Mercedes.''

''If you give me your list, I'll get you a copy,'' Mercedes said. Cassandra resisted the urge to toss the clipboard. She handed it to Mercedes instead. ''Would you like to discuss your selections with your mother first or should I have them entered into the computer?''

Cassandra couldn't go through this again. Picking out a place setting for dinners she and Troy would never share. Just thinking about it hurt. ''You can enter them into the computer.''

''I'll fax a copy to your mother,'' Mercedes said. ''You can make another appointment to pick out serving pieces, housewares and bedding. I'll be right back.''

As Mercedes walked away, Troy smiled. ''Now that wasn't so hard, was it?''

''No.'' It was too easy. Too easy to forget they were pretending. Cassandra felt engaged. She felt as if she was going to marry Troy. She wanted to marry Troy.

*She loved him. Truly loved.* Her stomach churned and did a somersault.

Troy touched the edge of her mouth. ''Smile, please. You look like you lost your best friend.''

She forced a smile. It wasn't easy. Whoever said it took more muscles to frown than smile was a damn fool.

''Is something wrong?'' he asked.

Wrong? Everything was wrong. What an idiot. Loving Troy even though she knew she shouldn't, knew she couldn't. They were too different. He was too much like Eric. Troy defined success by his career, by the amount of money, power and prestige he could achieve. His priorities were not only different than hers, they were a hundred and eighty degrees apart. Beyond the physical attraction and chemistry, they had nothing in common. He was the wrong man for her.

What was she thinking? There wasn't a right man for her. She had to stop feeling this way; she had to stop loving him. She didn't want to get hurt; she didn't want to love anyone.

Getting away from Troy was her only chance. Getting away now. Staying away forever. "I want to cancel the engagement party."

His eyes widened. "You want to what?"

Staring into his eyes, Cassandra's resistance started to melt. Troy's thick-lashed, blue eyes should be on the FBI's list of deadly weapons. She would never be able to look him in the eyes and say no. Never. Cassandra looked at the marble-tiled floor instead. "I'm sorry, Troy, but I can't go through with it."

He grabbed hold of Cassandra's hand before she could step onto the next escalator and pulled her toward the dress department on the second floor. "Why don't I buy you a new dress? That will make you feel better."

Typical man. "Like a new dress will solve everything."

"Most women—"

She jerked her hand away. "I'm not most women, Troy."

"No, you're not," he said. "But I still want to buy you a dress for the party."

Hadn't he heard a word she'd said? She didn't want to love a man this stubborn. She didn't want to love any man. "Spend as much of your precious money as you want, but it's not going to change my mind. I don't want to go to the engagement party."

Troy released an exasperated sigh. "You make it sound like I'm trying to buy you."

"No, you're trying to change me." Oops. She hadn't meant to say that. She wasn't thinking straight.

"What's that supposed to mean?"

Cassandra walked over and pulled out a boring, black dress from a rack. "Let me guess, you want me to wear something like this with a string of pearls and a stylish pair of pumps."

"Is that so bad?"

Yes, she wanted to scream. That's how she used to dress. She'd escaped from everything Troy wanted to achieve. She'd tried that life and wanted nothing more from it. The investment world—Troy's world—left her cold. She would not return to it. Not for her family, not for Troy.

Even if she could come to terms and accept the life Troy wanted, he would never want her. He would never love her as she was. He would want her to go back to who she'd been.

Just like Eric. He'd traded her in for Emily, who was the definition of a suitable corporate wife—intelligent, beautiful, presentable. That's what Troy wanted, someone like Emily.

"Don't you see, it's not me. It would be a lie. Like our engagement and registering tonight." Knowing it would never be real caused an ache deep within Cassandra. She tucked a stray piece of hair behind her ear. "The engagement party would be another lie, and I'm tired of living a life full of lies. It's gone too far."

"I understand."

He couldn't understand; he couldn't know how she felt.

"We need to talk." Troy motioned to the nearby salesclerks staring at them. "Someplace more private."

Sitting on a bench in Union Square, Cassie glanced at a lighted Nike billboard. "Do you think the 49ers will win on Sunday?"

"Don't change the subject." Troy wasn't about to let her do that. "I don't care about the 49ers or football right now."

"Your choice."

"I'm glad you're finally seeing things my way."

She stared at a crowded cable car headed down Powell Street. The driver clanged the bell and passengers waved. Must be tourists.

"Tell me why you want to cancel the engagement party."

A strong gust of wind made Cassie shiver so Troy put his arm around her. "I don't want to talk about it."

"Too bad. I want to discuss it."

"Are you always so…pushy?"

"Only when I have to be."

"I think it would be for the best," she said, her vague answer telling him nothing.

"You're going to have to do better than that."

She took a deep breath. "Registering made me realize we've taken this pretend engagement too far. I want it to stop."

"It will stop after the party."

"I want everything to stop now, before I..."

"Before you what?"

She hesitated. "Before we make it worse than it already is."

"But the party—"

"Means a lot to you. I know, Troy," she said with sincerity. "I wish I could help you."

"You can." Troy wished he knew what was going on inside her beautiful head. He sensed her uncertainty. "Be my fiancée."

"It's not that simple," Cassie said. "The party will be a total nightmare, and I know Emily will pull something."

"Is she the reason you want to cancel the party?"

"Partly." She tapped her foot against the pavement. The syncopated rhythm matched his own heart rate. "Remember when I told you my parents put stars on my ceiling?"

Troy nodded, remembering well. Wishing on a plastic star, the closeness of that night. The next morning, he'd thought it would disappear in the harsh reality of day. But it hadn't. "Your mother was worried about you getting cold."

"That wasn't the real reason," Cassie said. "They did it because they were worried about kidnappers."

"Kidnappers?"

"Being rich isn't all fun and games. One night, someone tried to kidnap me when I'd gone to the beach to stargaze."

The thought of anything happening to Cassie made his gut tighten. Troy pulled her close. He never wanted to let go of her. Never.

After a few seconds, Cassie pulled away. "Would you mind if we headed to the truck? It's getting cold."

Troy wanted to keep holding her, but Cassie had already stood. "Let's go."

"The only reason the kidnapping attempt failed is my father had a bodyguard following me. Emily and I had bodyguards, but we didn't know it."

She licked her lips. "After that night, things got pretty bad. I was the rebellious one, the one who didn't follow the rules. My parents didn't blame me, at least not to my face, but I saw how it haunted them. I felt like I owed them so I tried to be everything they wanted me to be."

"And?"

"And it made them happy. I did everything I was supposed to do. Of course, Emily got angry. She was no longer the only perfect daughter. She even accused me of setting up the kidnapping attempt so I'd get more attention than she would."

"Sibling rivalry?"

"To the extreme. I thought the competitiveness would disappear when we got older. A few years ago, I realized I wasn't happy with the person I'd become and I'd lost the real me, so I changed my life. Goodbye perfect daughter, hello black sheep of the family." Cassandra pressed the crosswalk button. "I thought that would solve my problems with Emily. It had. Until Eric.''

Crossing the street, Troy took Cassie's hand in his. He didn't know what else to do.

"Three weeks before Eric and I were to get married, I found him.''

Was Eric lost? Troy didn't understand. "Found him?''

"In bed, my bed, with Emily.''

*In her own bed.* How could Emily do that to her own sister, her twin sister? And Eric, the so-called fiancé. Inexcusable.

No wonder Cassie didn't want to date anyone. She wore her heart on her sleeve. Wainwright had ripped it off and displayed it like a trophy. *What an idiot.*

Troy wanted to shove his fist down Eric's throat. "Cassie.''

"I wasn't spying or anything like that,'' she said, as they entered the Stockton-Sutter garage. "I almost wish I had been, but I had no idea. That's what made me feel so foolish, so stupid. All of the signs were there, but I didn't see them. Didn't want to see them.''

Troy kissed the top of her hand. "You don't have to tell me this.''

"I want to, so you'll understand.'' She squeezed his hand, the simple gesture touching his heart. "That morning, I had forgotten some bills when I left for work. After Moe arrived, I ran home to get the envelopes. I was about to leave when I heard laughter coming from the bedroom. I was so shocked. I almost walked into the room when I saw them, but my feet wouldn't move. When Eric told Emily he would dump me and marry her, I ran out of the apartment before they saw me."

The ultimate betrayal. "You never confronted them?"

"No." Cassie's lower lip trembled. "I broke up with Eric that night. I moved out of the apartment the next day and donated the bed to a women's shelter."

"I thought he broke—"

"So does everyone, including Emily. They waited three months before announcing their engagement. I guess they didn't want to flaunt it in my face."

Troy hugged her. Her family thought Eric had dumped her. In some ways he had, but Cassie had had the last word. She would never be any man's doormat. Troy respected that. "Three months isn't a long time."

"It was long enough for them," she said without a trace of bitterness or regret. "I've gotten over Eric. I would never have been happy married to him. I realize that now. He was more interested in working with my father, than loving me. And I never loved him the way I..." Cassie bit her lip.

"Are you okay?"

She nodded. "What Emily did hurt most of all. We've always been competitive and different, but I felt so betrayed. We shared my mother's womb for nine months, you'd think that would count for something."

Five minutes alone with Wainwright. That's all Troy wanted. And Emily. Maybe cutting up her charge cards would do the trick. "I wish I could say or do—"

"I don't want you to do anything," Cassie interrupted. "I wanted you to know, that's all. I don't ever want to get hurt like that again. I don't think I could handle it. Just like I don't think I can handle the engagement party."

Troy raised her chin with his fingertip. "I would never purposely hurt you, Cassie."

The edges of her mouth turned up slightly. "I needed to hear you say that."

He brushed his lips against hers. "Then I'll say it again."

"About the party?"

The party. He wanted to ask her to change her mind, but he couldn't. Not tonight, possibly not ever. He needed time to think. Time to understand his growing feelings toward Cassie.

"We can talk about it tomorrow." Troy paid the parking lot attendant and received an exit ticket. "Right now, I should take you home."

## 9

The next morning, Troy sat behind his desk. He'd been reading the same piece of paper for the last twenty minutes, but hadn't comprehended a single word. Not even the catch phrase "wireless communications" managed to excite him.

For the first time ever, he wanted to take a day off. Call it a mental health day or a vacation day, he didn't want to work. He wanted to be with Cassie.

Leaning back in his chair, Troy set the letter on his desk. He'd been thinking about Cassie all morning. Thinking he wanted to keep seeing her after they called off their "engagement." It didn't make sense, but Troy didn't care. She might not be perfect, but maybe perfect was overrated. She was beautiful and good for him. With Cassie, he could loosen up, relax. Funny how being with her made him feel free, more alive than ever.

Last night had been only the beginning. She'd opened up to him, sharing her secrets. He wanted to know more; he wanted to know everything about her. Troy didn't understand his feelings, but he felt an overwhelming urge to protect her. Canceling the engagement party was the only solution.

So what if he missed out on meeting and partying

with the movers and shakers of Silicon Valley? There would be time for that later, once he had his partnership.

His phone rang once, signaling an internal call, and he picked up the receiver. "Troy McKnight."

"Can you come to Mick's office?" Della, Mick's secretary asked. "He wants to see you, now." She emphasized the last word.

"Be right there." Troy grabbed a notepad and a pen, thankful for the distraction. Mick would get him motivated to do some work.

The door to the office was open. Troy glanced in. Mick stood in front of his desk, dressed in a navy pin-striped suit and flashy purple tie. He smiled, waving him inside. "Have a seat, Troy."

He sat in a comfortable leather chair. Mick leaned against his desk. "I want to congratulate you."

*Yes. I got the partnership.* No reason to have the engagement party now. Troy could tell Cassie to cancel it without a second thought. Both of them would be happy. Troy clenched his hand into a fist and pumped it slightly.

"Of course, my wife wanted to know why I kept your engagement a secret. Heather was thrilled when she found an invitation to your engagement party in our mailbox."

Damn. No partnership. Yet. "I hope you can come." He hoped the answer was no.

"We wouldn't miss it," Mick said. "Though I was a little surprised. With all the long hours you put in, I didn't know you were dating anyone, let alone engaged."

"Cassie understands about my job."

"I'm sure she does." Mick grinned. "I'm looking forward to meeting her and so are the other partners."

"Other partners?"

"They'll be coming to the engagement party, too."

Damn. Canceling the engagement party would be tricky, but Troy had to do it. He had to think of Cassie and her happiness. But all the partners? Dammit. "I can't wait for everyone to meet Cassie, either."

"Have you set a wedding date?"

"Not yet." Troy pictured Cassie in a wedding gown and a flower-filled church. He liked the image, including a barefoot bride. Maybe it was time he took life less seriously, lightened up a little. "Maybe April."

"Keep me posted, will you? Heather's going to want to know all the details. You know how women are."

Troy nodded, relieved Cassie wasn't one of those women who lived for gossip, shopping and weddings.

Mick rubbed his hands together. "How would you like to go with me to visit InterTalk?"

InterTalk? The Austin firm was one of the hottest start-ups around. InterTalk was creating digital imaging and audio technology and group ware—from video conference calls and video chat rooms via the Internet to other collaborative software that had investors salivating. "They turned us down."

Mick smiled. "That was before we teamed up with Daniels Venture Group."

Teamed up with Dixon's group? Troy's heart fell to his feet.

"Dixon and I had several long telephone conversations recently. He has approached us with a unique opportunity."

Us? Troy still didn't feel any relief. His collar seemed to be shrinking by the second.

"He's giving us the chance of a lifetime, and I want you in on the deal."

"Thanks." *I think.*

"To be honest, Troy. Serious questions have been raised about making you a partner in the new fund."

It couldn't get any worse than this. He tugged on his collar.

"Experience counts, but contacts and connections are invaluable."

It was worse. He swallowed the lemon-size lump lodged in his throat. If he choked to death, he wouldn't have to worry about the engagement party.

"Of course, none of us knew you had Dixon Daniels in your corner," Mick said. "And it is something we will take into serious consideration. We don't want to lose you to Dixon and his group."

Troy's partnership wasn't dead, but he would have to go through with the engagement party. He didn't have a choice. Surely Cassie would understand. And they would have to be the perfect couple, a couple on parade. Cassie was not going to be happy. Not at all. "I've enjoyed working here."

"Glad to hear it," Mick said. "Of course, getting married and starting a family are life-altering events, you'll have to consider all of your options."

Options? Troy knew one option he had—to return to his parents' farm. He imagined cold, rainy days, mud and manure-soaked jeans and aching muscles. Returning home meant admitting defeat. "I do have my future to consider."

"This deal will be a good experience for you, Troy. You'll be working with me and Dixon."

Working with Dixon Daniels. It was like a minor leaguer getting batting tips from Barry Bonds. But Troy didn't feel lucky. He would need to swallow an entire bottle of Tums to make it through the rest of the day.

And what would happen after the engagement party? After he and Cassie were no longer engaged?

Troy imagined butchering a chicken for his mother and harvesting crops with his father. He tried to convince himself it wouldn't be the end of the world if he had to return to the farm, but couldn't. If he returned home without making the millions he'd touted about when he left, he would return home a failure. Hell, his life would be a living hell.

Mick cracked his knuckles. "Of course, it's going to be busy until we leave on Sunday."

"Long hours don't bother me."

"What about your fiancée?"

"Cassie is extremely supportive. She runs her own business and understands the necessity of putting in extra hours." The words sounded like total B.S. but Mick seemed satisfied.

"She sounds like quite a woman."

"She is."

But how would Cassie feel when he told her they couldn't cancel the engagement party? Maybe flowers would help. He could have them delivered to the bookstore. No, she would see it as a bribe. And it would be. She deserved better.

"Don't look so worried." Mick patted Troy's shoulder. "I'll have you home in time for your party on Saturday night."

"Great." Troy tried to muster some enthusiasm. He should be happy; he should be ready to go. But he wasn't. Maybe the plane would break down and he wouldn't make it back in time. Maybe a big earthquake would strike…

"You know, Troy. I always knew you were ambitious, but I didn't know how badly you wanted it. I considered you our farm boy from Missouri, but I see I was way off base." Mick chuckled. "Marrying Dixon Daniels's little girl. I didn't know you had it in you."

Neither did Troy.

As the front door to Cassandra's Attic opened, a bell jingled. Cassandra smiled to greet her customer, but her smile faded when Troy walked in, wearing his navy suit—the one he'd worn the night they'd met.

"Hello." The sound of his voice covered her arms in goose bumps. She should turn up the heat.

"Shouldn't you be at work? What are you doing here?" The questions tumbled from her mouth, bypassing her brain. Her cheeks warmed. "What I meant to say is hello."

Troy's charming smile made Cassandra sag against the front counter. Could she spell *s-w-o-o-n?* Or *s-t-u-p-i-d?*

"The answers to your questions are yes, and I wanted to give you this." He handed her a white box of See's candy.

"Thanks." She opened the box and popped a chocolate into her mouth. Almost as tasty as Troy. Wait a minute. She didn't want to think about tasting Troy. After a sleepless night of thinking about him and feeling so vulnerable, she'd decided not to see him again. But here he was. Damn him.

"A midday visit during the week and a box of

candy?'' Something was up. She drew her eyebrows together. ''What's going on?''

He shoved his hand into his pocket and jiggled some change. ''Nothing.''

She didn't buy it. Not with the way he kept glancing around the empty bookstore. ''No one is here, except you and me. Don't tell me you took time from your busy work schedule to make a social call?''

''I have to go to Austin for an important meeting.''

''You came all the way over here to tell me you're going on a business trip?''

''Yes.'' Troy hesitated. ''And to say I'll be back in time for the party Saturday night.''

Was she in the middle of an ''X-Files'' episode or did Troy suffer a lapse of amnesia? ''Don't you remember what I told you last night? There isn't going to be an engagement party.''

''Cassie, I heard everything you said, and I was going to tell you to cancel the party, but then I spoke with my boss.'' Troy paused. ''Mick and the other partners were invited. They're looking forward to attending. I'm on the verge of getting a partnership. I need to show them I... Cassie, please.''

Back to business. It always came down to his job. No matter how much she wanted it to be different, it wasn't. Troy wasn't.

Nothing last night had been real, nothing last weekend, either. Not his mind-blowing kisses. Not the security being in his arms brought her. Not the ease with which she could talk with him. Nothing. And it hurt. Because it seemed real. Because she wanted it to be real.

''I won't have time to take you shopping for a dress.''

"Is that supposed to make me feel better?"

"No," he admitted. "But it was worth a shot. What do you say?"

Say? She wanted to protect her heart and herself. She wanted to keep her feelings under control, ignoring any romantic notions. She wanted to sound annoyed and tell Troy McKnight good riddance. But it was so hard when she wanted to agree with him and melt in his mouth like one of the chocolates. Hadn't she learned her lesson yet? She bit her lip.

*Tell him no.*

Cassandra liked being alone; she was comfortable being alone. So what if she also liked being with Troy? He wasn't good for her; he wasn't what she needed.

*What if he is?*

Troy handed her a chocolate-covered cherry. "Pretty please with a cherry on top."

One look in his blue eyes and she was lost. Again. "Okay, but I'm going to regret this."

"No, you won't." He walked behind the counter. "Thank you, Cassie."

"Don't thank me," she said, angry at herself for being such a wimp. A store full of self-help and relationship books and she'd caved in because of a pair of baby blue eyes. Pathetic. Instead of asserting herself, she was agreeing to go to an engagement party when she wasn't engaged. Crazy. Cassandra wondered if Dr. Laura would consider this one of the ten stupid things women do to mess up their lives. "Just promise to visit me when they cart me off. I must be insane for agreeing."

"Why?"

"You're getting everything your heart desires—a

partnership, introductions to high-powered players, everything. I'm getting nothing, zip, zilch."

*Except a massive headache and a broken heart.*

"I'll make it up to you."

*You can't.* "I'm not going to wear black."

"Okay." He moved closer. "Wear purple."

Staring at the width of his shoulders, she gripped the counter. "I'm not going to wear a strand of pearls, either."

"Wear crystals."

Did he have to stand right next to her? She ignored the urge to nuzzle her face against his neck and inhale his intoxicating scent. "And I'm not going to wear my hair in a French twist."

"Do what you want with your hair." Troy put his arms on her shoulders. "And I will make this up to you. I promise."

The color of his eyes darkened to a midnight blue. He wanted to kiss her; she wanted him to kiss her. Again and again.

A warning sounded in her brain. Listening to it would be the smart thing to do, but she turned it off instead. She didn't want to follow reason. She wanted to ignore common sense, forget all about the consequences of her actions. Might as well have *F-O-O-L* tattooed across her forehead.

Troy lowered his mouth to hers. He kissed her gently as if testing her reaction. But Cassandra didn't want gentle. She wanted all of him. Opening her mouth wider, she pressed harder against his lips.

Pulsating sensations of pleasure raced through her, erasing any lingering doubts about what she was doing. She wanted this, wanted this now.

Troy deepened his kiss, ravishing her lips with a

hunger she understood. So good. Cassandra arched against him. She wanted only to taste Troy, to feel him.

*This isn't real. He isn't real.* She ignored the blurt of reality.

She no longer knew the definition of real. Troy's kisses felt real; he felt real.

The bell on the front door rang. Troy pulled away from her so quickly, she nearly lost her balance. A woman pushing a baby stroller entered the bookstore.

"We both need to get back to work," Troy said. "I'll call you."

Don't bother, Cassandra wanted to scream, but didn't. She couldn't. Not with the liquid heat running through her veins. Not when the desire in Troy's eyes matched her own. Not when she wanted him, wanted him badly. She touched her fingertip to her tingling lips.

Maybe his trip to Austin was a blessing. A separation would do them good. After the engagement party, the separation would be forever. And it was time for her to start facing the music. She might be able to put off reality for another week, but after the party Cassandra would have to face facts.

A relationship with Troy wasn't going to work.

Sitting on her futon couch, Cassandra tried reading a bestselling legal thriller, but she couldn't get past the third page. She glanced at the clock. Eleven o'clock. It was past midnight in Texas. And Troy hadn't called her yet. Every night for the past week, he had called. Sometimes the calls were short, other times long. It didn't matter to Cassandra. She liked hearing Troy's voice and talking to him over the phone was safer than being together. And separated by the miles, they were becoming friends.

Only it was too late.

One more night until the engagement party. Only one more night until it was over.

Cassandra ignored the jagged pain that sliced her heart every time she thought about saying goodbye to Troy. Even though she knew it was for the best, her heart had different ideas.

The buzzer to her apartment rang. Who would be ringing her doorbell at this hour? Maybe her neighbor's cat, Macy, had run away again.

Carrying her book, she padded her way to the door. "Who is it?"

"Who do you think?"

Troy. Her pulse picked up speed. She unlocked and opened the door. He held a bouquet of roses, lilies, daisies and heather. "Hi."

"Hi." She sounded breathless, but Cassandra didn't care. Staring into Troy's eyes, which were fringed with thick, lush lashes, made her breathless. She clutched her book so she wouldn't drop it.

"Sorry to drop by so late, but my flight was delayed. I took a shuttle from the airport." He handed her the flowers.

The floral scent filled the air. "They're beautiful." *Just like you.* Even though his suit was wrinkled, his tie loosened and his hair a mess, he looked gorgeous.

"Can I come in?"

Cassandra caught her breath. "I'm sorry, come in."

He carried in his garment bag and briefcase and set them inside the door next to a stack of new hardback books. He also removed his jacket and tie and tossed them onto the patchwork-quilt-covered futon.

"This place is great." Troy looked around. "It fits you."

"Thanks." Her flat was old, but had so much character with its high ceilings, hardwood floors, picture rails and a bay window. Thanks to inexpensive treasures found at garage sales and thrift stores, she'd made herself a comfy home. A bit cluttered and mismatched, but Cassandra loved it. Troy seemed to like it, too. She remembered the flowers in her hand. "I need to put these in water."

"Where did you find the color for the walls?"

Cassandra grabbed a blue vase from the top of the refrigerator. "I took a mango to the hardware store, cut it open and had them match the color."

He grinned. "That is so…you. I need you to help me liven up my apartment. Compared to this place, it's as homey as a morgue."

"Just tell me when." She filled the vase with water and arranged the flowers.

"Did you work until closing tonight?" Troy asked from the bar separating the kitchen from the living room.

"No," she said, not wanting to admit she'd left early in case he called. "Moe closed up."

Troy drew his brows together. "He doesn't mind working at night?"

"No, his boyfriend works at a restaurant so he prefers working nights."

"Moe's boyfriend?"

"Yes." She noticed the confused look in Troy's eyes. "Do you have a problem with that?"

"No." He chuckled. "Not at all."

Cassandra didn't understand the joke. He couldn't

be jealous, could he? The thought made her pulse race. Moe would get a real kick out of that, too.

"I hope your week went better than mine." Cassandra carried the vase of flowers into the living room. She'd left her book in the kitchen. She was done reading for tonight.

"What happened?"

She pushed aside a stack of *Publishers Weekly*s and set the vase on the coffee table. "You know how I wanted a fiancé so they would leave me alone."

"Yes."

"Well, my family is bugging me more than ever. My mother calls daily with wedding suggestions. Emily calls to talk about the engagement party. Even Eric has to give his advice." Cassandra sighed. "The past few days have been a nightmare."

Troy squeezed her shoulder. "We'll get through this."

The warmth of his touch penetrated the fabric to her skin. She wished he wouldn't let go of her. Ever. "Only one more night to go."

"I wanted to talk to you about that," Troy said.

No wonder he brought flowers. Another bribe? "We aren't going to keep pretending after tomorrow night."

"I'm tired of pretending, too. But come Sunday, I still want to be around. For real."

Her palms felt sweaty; her heart pounded in her throat. "What if I don't want you around?"

"Try to get rid of me."

Those were the words she wanted to hear. She didn't know what to say herself.

"I missed you, Cassie."

"I missed you, too." She fought the urge to twirl around the room. "Would you like a drink?"

Flashing her a flirtatious smile, he pulled her close. "The only thing I want to taste is you. I haven't been able to stop thinking about kissing you. But I only want that if you do."

Too late to turn back. Nothing less than a 7.0 earthquake would stop her now. It made little sense, but she was past the point of caring. She wanted him; she intended to have him.

She kissed him in reply, exploring his mouth, feeling the different textures, tasting his warmth. She ran her fingers through his soft, curly hair.

Greedy for more, Cassandra cupped his bottom. She pushed him closer to her. He wanted her. The evidence pressed against her belly. She wanted him, too. Right here, right now. She smiled.

"Is something funny?" Showering kisses along her neck and behind her ears, he rubbed his hands over her back, kneading and massaging her muscles.

"No." His kisses turned her legs to mush. She supported herself against him. "I was wondering if my back was up to another night on a hard floor."

With little effort, Troy picked her up. "Which way to your bedroom?"

She felt so safe, so secure with his strong arms holding her. Pointing to the doorway, she batted her eyelashes. "I love a man who takes control of a situation."

"Sweetheart." Troy captured her mouth in another earth-shattering, intoxicating kiss that made her want to give up all control, forever. "You ain't seen nothing yet."

"Is that a promise, my McKnight in shining Armani?"

"It's a guarantee."

Cassandra could hardly wait. Whatever happened would be fine by her. Tonight was all that mattered. She nibbled on his ear, inhaling the male scent that was uniquely his.

In the bedroom, he set her on the bed. Staring up at him, she read the desire in his eyes, desire for her. None of their differences would get in the way here.

With skilled hands, Troy unbuttoned the front of her dress. Focusing all his attention on her, he made Cassandra forget everything except here and now. She felt as if they were the only two people on earth, and this moment was their destiny.

Troy peeled the fabric off her shoulders, until the dress pooled around her waist, and kissed her bare skin. His lips blazed a trail of whisper-light kisses down her neck, past her collarbone, leaving her speechless. Cassandra shivered.

As his fingers followed the same path, goose bumps covered her arms. She'd never noticed before, but his fingertips were rough, callused perhaps from working on the farm. And she loved the way they made her feel.

Cassandra never knew gentle kisses and caresses could be so stimulating. Troy was making love to her with his warm, strong hands and his soft, moist lips. She didn't need champagne, candlelight or music for an evening of romance. She only needed Troy. She leaned her head back.

With a flick of his fingers, her lacy underwire bra sprang open, releasing her swollen breasts. He pushed her straps off her shoulders. "You are so beautiful."

Troy made her feel beautiful. He cupped one of her breasts in his hand, then lowered his mouth to her nipple. Torturing her with his tongue, he created a longing for fulfillment that couldn't wait. She shuddered, feeling the heat, the pleasure radiating through her entire body. "Troy."

She lifted her hips so he could pull her dress over them. He took the liberty of helping her out of her black tights and shoes. She wore only a wisp of lace panties.

The way he stared at her with such desire made her feel sexy, alive.

*I love you, Troy McKnight.*

The thought was so clear, so loud, she wondered if she'd said the words aloud. He reached for her panties, but she stopped him. He was still fully dressed. She wanted to make him feel the way she did. "Your turn."

As she kissed him long and hard, Cassandra undid half the buttons on his shirt, pulling the ends out of his pants. No sense wasting time. She yanked the shirt over his head.

Unable to resist the impulse, she sprinkled kisses down his chest to his belly button. She ran her hands along his back, feeling the muscular ridges. It was his turn to experience the torture of those overwhelming sensations. She drew circles with her tongue on his nipples until they hardened in response.

"Cassandra, stop."

She didn't stop, but increased her speed until he moved back. "You're driving me crazy."

She couldn't get enough of him. "Now you know how I feel."

With amazingly steady hands, she unclasped his

belt, then unzipped his pants. Troy kicked off his shoes. Cassandra helped him out of his pants and peeled off his socks. He stood in front of her wearing a pair of flannel plaid boxers, his arousal evident.

Slipping her hands under the elastic band, she pushed his boxers off and stared at him. Sheer perfection. She wanted to touch and kiss every inch of his glorious body. So she did, feeling no hesitation or shyness.

Troy moaned. He kissed her, slipping his hand under the lace. Again his fingers worked their magic. Each touch sent electric shock waves through her body. He kissed her again, stroking her until she couldn't think any longer, until her body ached with a need so great she thought she would cry. "I want you now."

"Not yet."

What? She was hot and wet and ready. She didn't want to wait. "Please."

"First." Troy pushed her panties over her hips. He smiled mischievously. "I want to find your tattoo."

# 10

The next morning, Troy opened his eyes. Rays of sunlight glinted off Cassie's golden hair, which covered his chest like a satin sheet. She snuggled closer, her body warm and soft. Beautiful.

Feeling more content than he ever had, he cupped her well-rounded bottom with his hand. Lightly, he stroked the spot where he'd found her delicate rose tattoo last night.

How did he get so lucky?

Cassie was a gorgeous, passionate woman. So what if they were different? The differences in their personalities complemented each other. His stability kept her from floating away like a helium balloon let loose in the sky; her vivacity lifted him enough to keep his feet from being cemented too firmly on the ground. And physically—Troy sighed—she fit him perfectly, as if she'd been made only for him. After last night's lovemaking marathon, Troy could almost believe she had been.

Stirring, Cassie blinked her eyes open. ''Good morning.''

She traced hearts on his chest with her fingertips. Her gentle touch started building a heat in his groin.

Troy massaged one of her shoulders. Her moan sounded more like a kitten's purr. He could get used to this, easily.

"Did you sleep well?" she asked with a satisfied smile.

Considering he'd hardly slept, he felt unbelievably rested. "Yes, I did."

"Good." She crawled on top, straddling him. "Because you're going to need all your energy."

The small heat erupted into a fire. His blood surged. She lowered her mouth to his.

The phone rang. *Not now.*

Cassie stared at the phone.

"Don't answer it." Trying to distract her, he kissed her neck.

The phone rang again.

"Troy, please." She tried to move off him, but he held her so she couldn't. "It could be an emergency at the bookstore."

"Let the machine get it."

The phone rang again.

"I have to answer it." Cassie reached over to pick up the receiver. "Hello... No, I was awake, Emily. It's almost nine-thirty."

More than a little frustrated, Troy looked at the ceiling. Why did Cassie always have to pick times like now to be responsible? She could be so unpredictable, but that's what he loved about her.

Loved?

Where had that come from? Troy stared at her with new awareness. He was falling in love with her. Hell, tumbling downhill was a more apt description. The thought made him smile. Things just might work out.

"Really." She moved off him. "I didn't know they went, too... He did?" She drew her brows together until two small lines formed above her nose. "No."

The color of her eyes deepened. "You can come over if you want, but I can dress myself. No, Troy won't be here."

Where was he going? He touched her arm. Cassie shook his hand off. What the hell?

"Okay, if you insist. I'll see you then." She covered herself with the comforter. "Bye."

Cassie hung up the telephone and took a deep breath. "That was Emily. She told me you were in Austin with Daddy and Eric."

Nodding, Troy reached over to uncover her breasts.

She crossed her arms in front of her chest, stopping him. "Why didn't you tell me?"

"I was going to tell you."

Her nostrils flared. "When? After you went to work for my father?"

Troy brushed his hand through his hair. "We are only working on a deal together. One deal, honey."

"Don't call me that."

"Cassie—"

"Emily said my father offered you a job."

"I didn't accept it."

"Did you say no?"

Troy hadn't. It was a dream offer. One he didn't want to turn down. "Not yet."

"Why?"

"Because I wanted to discuss the offer with you." He held her hand. "Cassie, I should have told you last night, but I had something else on my mind."

She jerked her hand away. "Like seducing Dixon Daniels's daughter?"

"I had you on my mind, nothing else." Her reaction angered him. How could she accuse him of seducing her? She had been more than a willing participant. "You're not being fair."

"What you did wasn't fair." She gritted her teeth. "Using our engagement, using me."

Troy rolled his eyes. "This deal has nothing to do with you and me."

"But the job offer does."

"I didn't solicit your father for a job. He offered."

"You used me." Her voice cracked. "You used me to get close to my father. I should have known better. Thinking someone like you could love someone like me."

Troy did love her, but if he told her now she wouldn't believe him. "If I wanted to use you, don't you think I would have slept with you in Carmel? I had the opportunity if you recall."

She squeezed her eyes shut. "I think you should go."

"Not until I've had my say."

Her eyelids flew open. "There's nothing you can say. I trusted you, Troy. I really did." Her bottom lip quivered. "I should've known you were no different than Eric."

Cassie had no right to compare him to her worthless ex-fiancé and brother-in-law.

"Wait a minute," Troy said. "If you trusted me, you wouldn't be saying any of this. You'd know I wouldn't use you. Why does everything have to be so black-and-white with you?"

"Because it's easier that way."

He sighed.

"You must be pleased with yourself. Eric had to sleep with both Emily and me to get what he wanted. You only had to sleep with me."

"Please don't take this to the extreme, Cassie. I'm not Eric."

She stuck her nose in the air. "If you say so."

Troy didn't need this. "Let's get a few facts straight. You're the one who approached me and asked me to pose as your fiancé. I wasn't hiding anything from you. I didn't ask for any of this. I didn't want any of this."

She gripped the comforter. "But you aren't complaining about what it's gotten you, are you?"

"Cassie, don't." She didn't understand; she didn't know he loved her. "I—"

Her lips tightened. "Don't apologize and don't worry about the engagement party."

"I don't care about the party, Cassie."

"Yes, you do. Don't worry, I won't jeopardize your hard work and your precious career. I'll be the perfect fiancée. But as soon as the party is over, I never want to see you again."

She couldn't mean it. He would give her a few minutes to calm down, give himself a couple, too. Troy put on his shirt, then realized it was inside out. Reversing the shirt, he put it on again. He finished dressing while she stared at the wall. "Are we going to let a little misunderstanding come between us?"

"A little misunderstanding?" she asked. "This isn't little, Troy. This is about you and me using each other. Oh, yes, I admit my part in this whole charade."

"Believe me, Cassie, I'm not using you." He was running out of time. He couldn't walk out without letting her know how he felt. "I couldn't use you. I— I love you." He couldn't believe he'd said that.

Her eyes widened. "It doesn't matter, Troy."

"How can it not matter?"

"Because we want different things from life. We're different." Her eyes glistened with tears. She pounded her fist against the bed. "This proves it."

"We may be different, but not where it matters."

"You mean in bed?"

He was so close to getting everything he wanted. He couldn't give it up now. "Cassie—"

"My name is Cassandra."

The front door slammed. Cassandra wouldn't cry. Not over Troy. He didn't deserve her tears. Clutching the comforter on her bed, she poked a hole through the cotton fabric with her fingernails, but held her tears at bay.

What a fool she'd been. Again.

Hadn't she learned her lesson the first time thanks to Eric Wainwright? Falling in love only caused pain.

Why did she think falling for Troy would be different? Because she wanted to believe he was different. She wanted to believe she'd found her Prince Charming, her Mr. Right. But she'd been wrong.

Troy was no different from Eric, from any man. She was an easy target. She knew better than to think men like that would want her, could love her. She'd made the same mistake twice, falling for two men who had used her to get close to her father. No one with any career aspirations could resist the lure Dixon Daniels offered. Why would Troy resist?

It made sense now. The flowers, the earth-shattering lovemaking. Make that sex, she corrected herself.

Who cared about Troy McKnight anyway? She didn't need him; she didn't need any man. She had her bookstore; she had her own life. She would simply forget him. He'd fade from her memory like a poorly written novel. She simply needed a little time, say a hundred years.

Her McKnight in shining armor? What a joke. So what if she could still smell his intoxicating male scent? She would wash the sheets. So what if she missed having his warm body next to her? She would get a pet. So what if she'd never experienced pleasure of such mythic proportions before? She would get a— no, she wouldn't.

Cassandra brushed her hair behind her shoulder. She would be the woman Troy wanted her to be and get through the engagement party. She'd gotten hurt before and survived. Somehow, she would survive this.

Love. Troy said he loved her. She almost believed him; she wanted to believe him. But she couldn't. Not now.

She didn't want to love him; she wouldn't love him anymore.

Rubbing her eyes, Cassandra ignored the void inside her. An emptiness, as if a piece of her heart had walked out the door with Troy. But that was ridiculous. She was overreacting, that's all. A void. She tsked. It meant nothing. Nothing at all.

\* \* \*

Waiting for the bus, Troy leaned against a graffiti-covered wall and rubbed his chin. The sharp stubble dug into his fingertips. He needed a shave, a shower and clean clothes. Those were things he needed. He didn't need Cassie.

The bus stopped in front of him. Troy reached into his pocket. His empty pocket. All of his change belonged to the man selling flowers at the airport newsstand. His wallet was in his jacket, and his jacket was at Cassie's.

Damn. No money, no ATM card. The bus pulled away, leaving a trail of foul-smelling exhaust. He was tired, too tired to walk clear across town. Tired enough to sit and think for a while. Brushing his hand through his hair, he sat on a nearby step.

Things weren't turning out as he planned. He'd planned on being made a partner, becoming a millionaire and providing for his family. Sitting in a doorway like a bum wasn't part of his plan. Meeting and falling in love with Cassie wasn't part of his plan, either.

Troy wanted to get married and have children, but he had a definite image of the kind of woman who would make him a good wife. He wanted a woman who would be the perfect venture capitalist wife. A woman who would support his goals and be understanding about his work and fit in with the crowd.

Cassie was none of those things. Though beautiful and intelligent, she was also free-spirited and unpredictable. Conformity was a four-letter word to her. Cassie didn't fit his image, but he loved her. Was love enough?

An old man with a weather-beaten face and snow-white hair sat next to him. The man wore tattered, grungy clothes and carried an overloaded duffel bag. He needed a shower worse than Troy did. ''I haven't seen you around before, so I thought I'd warn you. Crazy Teddy sleeps in this doorway, but he shouldn't be back until later.''

''Thanks for the warning,'' Troy said.

''Nice pants.'' The old man touched the wrinkled fabric. ''You steal 'em?''

Troy wore Armani. The old man had taste. ''No.''

''Bad day, huh?''

''You could say that.''

''Wanna talk about it?''

''No.''

''Didn't think so.'' The old man buttoned his army issue jacket. ''Must have something to do with a woman. No one likes to talk about that.''

Another bus stopped. A stream of passengers unloaded. A yuppie-looking couple stared at Troy and the old man. The woman, wearing a combination of J. Crew and L.L. Bean, handed two bus transfers to Troy. ''Have a nice day,'' she said before rejoining her significant other.

Troy stared at the pieces of paper. ''You want one of these?''

The man smiled a toothless grin. ''This is my home. I don't need to go anywhere.''

Troy needed the transfer, but did an average homeless person need one? He didn't think so. ''I need to go home.''

''Where is that?''

Good question. Home wasn't his luxurious Marina

apartment with a view of the Palace of Fine Arts. Home wasn't his parents' farm. "I wish I knew."

"I'm happy here," the old man said. "More sun than other parts of the city. I used to live in the park, but that didn't work out."

Before Troy could say anything, a man in an expensive jogging suit strolled by. He wore a Walkman and hundred-dollar running shoes. He handed the old man a dollar. "Spend the money on food, not liquor."

"Thank you, kind sir." The old man gave a mock bow before handing the dollar bill to Troy. "You look like you need this more than me."

He didn't need the man's money. Troy had a bus transfer. He could get home on his own. What was he thinking? He had plenty of money in the bank, an IRA at one of the top mutual funds in the country and a great job. "I can't take your money."

"You look like a good kid." The old man pushed the dollar into Troy's hand. "Take the dollar and take some advice. Clean yourself up and get a job. Find a woman to love and make a home for yourself."

Troy could have all those things. "Sounds like good advice."

The old man nodded. "I had all of that once, but I let it slip away. You're young enough. You still have a chance."

Troy clutched the dollar in his hand. Suddenly this one bill felt more important than the millions he planned to make. "I'll try."

"And always remember where home is." The man's eyes focused on something Troy couldn't see. "I forgot. When I finally remembered, it wasn't there anymore."

\* \* \*

Cassandra rubbed concealer under her swollen, red eyes. She had to pull herself together. The party was in less than two hours. Checking her reflection, she realized she needed to do something with her hair. Talk about a bad hair day…

The doorbell buzzed.

Her heart leaped into her throat. She ran to open it, unsure of why her pulse raced. Emily, wearing flowing black pants and a matching bolero jacket, stood with a metallic cosmetic box and a set of hot rollers in her hands.

Not now. Cassandra didn't need this. "Why was it so important for you to come over?"

"This is the first party I'm throwing as Mrs. Eric Wainwright." Emily marched into the apartment and set her things on the floor. "Lots of VIPs will be there. I have to make a good impression and I want everything to be perfect."

"Including me."

Emily nodded. "Is that so bad, Cassandra?"

"No, it's…"

Her sister was the perfect wife. The kind of woman Troy wanted, needed. No wonder Eric had dumped her for Emily. Just like Troy would. Cassandra blinked back the tears.

Emily gave her a hug, an uncharacteristic hug that opened the spill gate of Cassandra's tears. "What's wrong?"

After a few minutes the tears subsided. "I'm sorry, Emily. I hope I didn't get your jacket all wet."

"I'm not worried about the jacket," Emily said. "Are you going to tell me what's going on or am I going to have to guess why Troy's luggage and suit jacket are sitting by your door and he's not here?''

"He forgot to take them with him." Cassandra hesitated. "It's over. We're over."

"No, it isn't." Emily placed her hands on her hips. "I'm not going to let a lovers' quarrel ruin my party."

"Don't worry, your party will go on as planned."

"Thank goodness. Daddy would kill me." Emily patted her chest. "I thought I was experiencing heart palpitations."

"Why would Daddy care?"

"The party was his idea, but for some reason he wanted me to throw it."

Cassandra didn't understand, but at the moment she didn't care. She cared only about Troy. If only...

"Do you want to talk about what happened?"

"Not really."

Emily walked to the kitchen. She grabbed a cucumber from the refrigerator and sliced it. "Lie down and put these on your eyes."

Cassandra lay on the futon with the cold cucumbers on her aching eyes. A drawer opened and closed. Water ran in the sink.

"Here you go." Emily placed a wet cloth on Cassandra's forehead. "Do you have any aspirin?"

"In the bathroom, but I don't want any."

"They're not for you," Emily said. A few minutes later, she returned to the living room. "Are you wearing the little blue thing on your bed?"

"Yes."

"The pearls you got for graduation would be perfect. And you should wear your hair up. I'll plug in the hot rollers."

Emily was being too nice, too understanding. Cassandra didn't know what to say. "Okay."

"Eric told me Troy talked about you all week."

"He did?" Cassandra hoped it were true. But it was too late. Her stomach tightened. She was going to be sick.

"Yes. The man's crazy about you." Emily sounded sincere.

"It'll never work." The words were for Cassandra's own benefit as well as Emily's.

"Why would you say that?"

*Because I've been there before. With Eric.* "We're too different. Troy doesn't want me. He wants me to be…"

"To be what?"

Cassandra stared at the seeds on the cucumber. "To be like you."

"I'll take that as a compliment. Though I can't imagine why he'd want that."

"You're everything I'm not," Cassandra said finally. "You dress stylishly, have a trendy hairdo, know the right things to say and when to say them. You don't stick out like a cast member of a freak show."

"I'm boring and stuffy. A little anal, too. Someone once called me a snob. Can you imagine?" Emily sighed. "You're like a butterfly or a breath of fresh air. You always have been. When we were growing up, you didn't notice or care how beautiful you were. Still do. And when you stopped rebelling and started behaving after the kidnapping…I couldn't compete. You were still you, but you were edging in on who I was. I hated that. I hated you."

Cassandra noticed the past tense of the verb. "Emily—"

"We're grown-ups now," Emily said. "Time to put our petty jealousies and competitiveness behind us."

Could it be so easy? "But, Eric—"

"Look, we can discuss this until we're blue in the face, but it won't change the past. We can't change the past. Agreed?"

Unsure of what to say, Cassandra hesitated. She'd always felt like the wronged party and never considered Emily's feelings in the matter. The least Cassandra could do was meet her sister halfway. It would be a start. "Agreed."

"Do you love Troy?"

"More than I thought possible," she admitted. Telling someone was such a release. Even if that someone was Emily. "But I don't want the same things he wants. I can't be the kind of woman he wants me to be."

"Then don't. Be who you are," Emily said.

Cassandra hadn't been enough for Eric; she wouldn't be enough for Troy. "Who I am isn't good enough."

"Then to hell with Troy McKnight. He doesn't deserve you."

"Emily, really," Cassandra said, shocked by her usually prim and proper sister.

Emily smiled. "You sounded like Mom when you said that."

"I know."

"Let me see how your eyes look." Emily took the cucumber slices and damp rag from her. "Much better. Now we need to get you dressed for the party. By

the time I'm finished, Troy will take one look at you
and either fall to his knees or run to the nearest exit.''

For a moment Cassandra had forgotten about the
party. ''Why are you doing all of this for me?''

''Because we're sisters,'' Emily said. ''And it's
about time we started acting like it.''

# 11

Troy paced the foyer of the Pacific Heights mansion, his steps sounding on the marble-tiled floor. Cassie was late. Not that promptness was one of her priorities. Still it worried him.

Was she coming to the party?

Or not?

He wanted her to come; he needed her to come.

If she didn't come…

The massive stained-glass door opened. A man and woman stepped inside.

Where was Cassie? The partners from his firm were already in the ballroom drinking the expensive liquor and eating the delicious-smelling hors d'oeuvres. So were half the other guests.

The door opened again. *Let it be her.* And it was.

As Cassie stepped inside, Troy sucked in a breath. No crystals, no broomstick skirts, no boots. But pearls. She wore a strand around her neck. He couldn't believe it. This was the woman he wanted her to be, always knew in his heart she could be. Two thin straps held up the ice blue material that floated above her knees as she moved. Elegant, but slightly daring. The dress showed the right amount of curves. Enough curves to send his blood rushing to places he didn't want it to go. "Cassie."

"Sorry I'm late."

*Always late, that was his Cassie.* "It was worth it. You look…incredible, stunning."

"Thank you." She wore her hair up, with a few curly tendrils framing her rosy cheeks. A single pearl graced each ear. She chuckled. "Nice tie."

She'd called him rigid, a stick-in-the-mud and a few other things. Well, maybe he was. But he wanted to show her he could be spontaneous so on his way to the party, he'd stopped at the Disney Store and purchased a Mickey Mouse tie. It wasn't much, but it was for her, for agreeing to attend. Troy smiled.

Now was the time to tell her. He put his hands on her bare shoulders. "Listen, Cassie, I've got to tell you—"

The door opened again. Dixon and Vanessa entered, followed by… What were they doing here?

Every muscle of Troy's tensed. "Mom, Dad."

His father laughed. "Our eldest child is having an engagement party and he's surprised we're here. Kids."

His mother kissed Troy's cheek. "Dixon invited us and sent us airplane tickets. Why didn't you tell us you were engaged?"

"I've been meaning to, but things have been rather hectic."

"I would say that's an understatement." His mother smiled. "Aren't you going to introduce us to your fiancée?"

"Mom, Dad, this is Cassandra Daniels." Troy forced the words from his dry throat. "Cassie, these are my parents, Paula and Bill McKnight."

Troy caught a moment of panic in Cassie's eyes, but she recovered quickly. Smiling, she extended her hand. "It's w-w-wonderful you could come. Troy's always talking about his family and life back on the farm."

His beaming father pumped her hand. "Welcome to the family, Cassie. You'll have to come see the farm for yourself. It's a great place to raise a family."

"Don't be so subtle, Bill." Paula gave Cassie a hug. "We are so happy to meet you."

Dixon stepped up. "Before we join the rest of the guests, this might be a good time to give the kids your surprise, Paula."

She removed a small black box from her purse and handed it to Troy. "Your father and I thought you might want this."

Troy opened the box. A one-carat solitaire gleamed against the black velvet. His grandmother's engagement ring. His chest tightened; he started to sweat.

Cassie's mouth formed an *O*. "It's...it's beautiful."

"It belonged to my mother, Troy's grandma," his father explained. "Put it on her finger."

Not now.

Not this way.

Not when it didn't mean anything.

"What are you waiting for, son?"

Troy stared into Cassie's startled eyes. He gave her trembling hand a gentle squeeze. This wasn't the way it was supposed to be. As he slid the ring onto her finger, she tensed. Her eyes glistened, and she blinked.

"Does it fit?" Vanessa and his mother asked at the same time.

Cassie showed the ring to the curious mothers. "Yes."

"Fantastic." Dixon patted Troy on the back. "Let's go inside. Everyone's waiting to congratulate the happy couple. And I bet Cassie wants to show her ring off to Emily."

The next two hours passed quickly. Everything he'd dreamed of was happening. Troy worked the room with Dixon at his side and spoke with the inner circle of Silicon Valley venture capitalists and CEOs. Even the partners from Troy's firm seemed a tad overwhelmed by the well-wishers at the party. Troy couldn't ask for anything more. A complete success. A perfect evening. Except...

For the misery in Cassie's eyes.

She stood next to his parents, staring at the fresco painted on the ceiling. This wasn't working. Cassie might look the part, but she was hating every minute. And if the way she kept the engagement ring hidden from sight meant anything...

Last night had been important to her, too. Otherwise none of this would have mattered. Troy made his way through the crowd and touched her arm. "We need to talk."

Cassie nodded and led him into the cloakroom. The heavy wooden door dulled the music and the conversation in the ballroom. "I wanted to talk to you, too. I'm sorry for how I acted, overreacted, this morning. It was easier for me to believe you'd use me, than to think you wouldn't."

*It was going to work.* "I should have told you what was going on. I'm sorry."

She stared at the parquet floor. "Looks like it's working out the way you wanted."

*For me, what about you?* He hesitated.

"Everything you want is waiting for you in the other room."

"Not everything," he admitted. This was his chance. "I want you."

Cassie bit her lip. "I want you, too."

Her words sent his heart soaring. He put his arms around her and kissed her. She tasted so sweet, so warm. And she was his, all his.

Gently she pushed him away. "I want you, but I can't be with you."

"I don't understand."

"This isn't an easy thing to say, but it's not going to work. I can't live your kind of life."

"Can't we compromise?"

"I—"

"You said you wanted me. What about love?"

"Love doesn't change the fact you are a venture capitalist. You want to network at parties like this. You want to make millions of dollars. You want the power and the prestige. I don't."

What did she expect him to do? Give everything up for her?

Troy McKnight was the hottest property around. He'd made the right contacts—impressed and awed them. He was a shoo-in for a partnership. It was all waiting for him. He could taste it; he could feel it. He couldn't stop now.

Could he?

Damn. He shouldn't feel guilty; he shouldn't feel dead as if his heart had stopped beating. He was on the verge of getting everything he ever wanted. Everything he had planned for.

How could Cassie expect him to give that up? "So it's either you or my work?" *My dreams.*

"I'm not asking you to make a choice."

She removed the engagement ring and handed it to him. Troy wouldn't take it. "I love you."

Cassie hesitated. "Sometimes love isn't enough. You need a woman who shares your dreams, who wants the same things as you. A woman who can make you happy. I'm not her."

He loved her.

He needed her.

He wanted to marry her.

"Yes, you are. You are *her*."

She forced the ring into his hand. "No, I'm not."

"It doesn't have to be all or nothing. We can work through this."

"I'm sorry, Troy, but I can't go back to that life. Not even for you."

"Successful relationships are about compromise. We have to at least try. Please, meet me halfway."

"I...can't."

And Troy couldn't do it alone. Damn.

Before he could stop her, Cassie returned to the party. The door closed behind her. Standing alone in the cloakroom, he stared at the ring in his hand. The diamond seemed duller now that it wasn't on Cassie's finger.

No stars to wish upon, no words left to say. A precious gift had been ripped out of his hands and Troy was at a loss about how to get it back. He remembered what the old man told him. "Never forget where your home is."

What happened when "home" didn't want you?

Standing on the balcony outside the ballroom, Cassandra stared at the lights on the Golden Gate Bridge.

She wanted to ignore the turmoil raging inside her. She wanted the fog rolling in to dull the knife-edged pain stabbing her heart every time she thought of life without Troy.

Should she have given him a chance? Should she have been more willing to take a chance herself? The questions plagued her.

A door closed behind her. The hair on the back of her neck stood up. She was no longer alone. *Troy.* It had to be him.

"Cassandra."

She didn't turn; she couldn't. She clutched the rail. The only sounds were the trickling water from the fountain in the corner, Troy's footsteps and her pounding heart.

He stood behind her, too close for her own good. His warm breath caressed the back of her neck. His arm brushed hers. The brief contact sent a spark shooting through her. She stepped aside.

"Aren't you cold out here?"

"No, I was…enjoying the view."

His gaze met hers. "It is lovely."

The intensity of his eyes sent a shiver down her spine. Cassandra had used all of her strength and courage to tell Troy she wouldn't make him happy, that he needed to find someone else. The disappointment in his eyes had torn her heart in two, but she was doing this for his own good. She couldn't be the woman he wanted. Troy could never love her as she was.

"Why are you out here all alone?"

She'd left the party because the string quartet was playing a familiar song. A song she'd heard when they registered. A song she'd imagined herself walking down the aisle to. "I wanted some fresh air."

"It's a little stuffy in there."

"Are you talking about the air or the stuffed shirts?"

"Both."

His answer surprised her. She ignored the twinge of regret creeping up her spine. Saying goodbye to Troy McKnight was what she needed to do. It was what Troy needed her to do.

"I want to talk to you."

No. She didn't want to hear what he had to say. One word and she might wind up in his arms. She might forget that she wasn't the woman for him, that he wasn't the man. "Why?"

He leaned against the edge of the balcony. "I was wondering if you were planning on hiring any more help at the bookstore."

Troy wanted to talk about her bookstore, now? Puzzled, she drew her eyebrows together. "I can always use help."

"Good."

She wrung her hands, fighting her nervousness. "Does someone need a job?"

"Yes, me."

"You?" This wasn't funny. She wet her lips. "You already have a job and an offer from my father."

"Not any longer."

"Stop playing games, Troy."

"This isn't a game, Cassandra." Troy held her hand. His warmth seeped into her skin and spread through her. "I thought about what you said. I'd rather have you than all the money in the world so I'm going to quit my job on Monday."

"But…" Those were the words she wanted to hear, but it was the last thing she expected to hear. "How can you do that? It's what you've wanted, what you've been working for all these years."

Troy shrugged.

Realization hit her, like an oak bookcase falling on top of her. "You'd give it up, you'd give everything up for me?"

He nodded.

She should be jumping for joy. Instead she felt guilty for taking away Troy's dream. "Isn't that a bit…much?"

"Maybe a little, but what choice do I have?"

"I don't know, but you can't sacrifice everything you've ever wanted. It wouldn't be fair."

"I don't care," he said. "I love you, Cassandra."

"I…" She couldn't let him do this. He would live to regret the decision. There had to be another way. But what? She had agreed to meet Emily halfway. And Emily's betrayal had been one of the most painful events in Cassandra's life. Maybe she would do the same with Troy. It was either that or… "What if we compromised?"

"That's a thought." Troy rubbed his chin. "But I didn't think you knew the meaning of the word."

"I didn't know I did," she admitted. "But I've been told compromise is the key to a successful relationship."

"Don't you think it might be a bit extreme?"

"Not when…"

Suddenly everything made sense. Troy was giving her a taste of her own medicine, making her see there wasn't only black or white, all or nothing, one way or another. Cassandra smiled. "You're too smart for your own good, Troy McKnight."

"Do you still want to compromise?"

"You better believe it." She bit her lip. "Let's see, I'll attend dinners and business functions with you if you attend—"

"Poetry readings and..."

"Yoga classes with me."

He grimaced. "Yoga?"

"It's negotiable." She grinned. "Think you can handle it?"

"Yes."

Cassandra sighed. "I can't believe I'll be dating a venture capitalist."

"You won't be dating me." Troy dropped to one knee. "I'm hoping you will marry me?"

Her nerve endings quivered; her blood tingled. She struggled for a breath. "For real?"

"For real." Troy took the ring out of his pocket. "I love you. I want to marry you."

"Yes." Tears of happiness welled in her eyes. "I love you."

Troy slipped the ring on her finger. Standing, he pulled her into his arms and kissed her. "No more nights, weekends or weeks. I'll be your fiancé for life."

"No, you won't," she said. "You'll be my husband for life."

With that, Cassandra kissed him, long and hard. No more pretend kisses. Only real ones from now on. "I think I'm going to like being engaged for real."

"Wait until we're married, Cassandra."

Staring at the diamond ring on her finger, she smiled. "Call me Cassie, and I don't want to wait."

She pushed back the sleeve of his jacket and read the time on his Rolex. "We should have long enough."

Troy grinned. "What did you have in mind?"

"Ever make love to your fiancée on a balcony before?"

"I, uh—"

"Me neither." She pulled on his Mickey Mouse tie until he was nose-to-nose with her. "I'm game if you are or we could sneak off and get matching tattoos."

Troy hesitated, but only for a moment. With a gentle caress, he slid the left strap of her dress off her shoulder. "We McKnights aim to please."

Cassie winked. "So is that a yes for the lovemaking or the tattoos?"

\* \* \* \* \*

# MILLS & BOON®

# *Makes any time special*

## *Enjoy a romantic novel from Mills & Boon®*

*Presents...™*  *Enchanted™*  TEMPTATION®

*Historical Romance™*  ⊣ MEDICAL ROMANCE®

# MILLS & BOON®

## *Presents...*™

**THE CATTLE KING'S MISTRESS** by *Emma Darcy*

Nathan King, powerful head of his family's cattle empire, is wary about getting too involved with elegant beauty, Miranda. He's certain she won't be able to cope with outback life. Yet the passion between them is overwhelming...

**THE PERFECT FATHER** by *Penny Jordan*

In a moment of weakness, Samantha had confessed that she yearned to become a wife and mother. Liam had always thought her impetuous nature made them an unlikely match. But suddenly he found himself wanting to succumb to Samantha's tantalising sensuality...

**THE ITALIAN SEDUCTION** by *Mary Lyons*

Antonia knew that being Lorenzo Foscari's bodyguard was going to be hard work. But, after he kissed her, she found that guarding his body—day and night—could be more of a pleasure than she'd ever imagined...

**BOUND BY CONTRACT** by *Carole Mortimer*

Actress Madison had been contracted to live and work with demanding film director, Gideon Byrne, for eight months! She was irresistibly attracted to him, even though she knew he would sack her if he discovered her true identity...

### *Available from 2nd June 2000*

# MILLS & BOON®

## *Presents...*™

### MARRIAGE FOR REAL *by Emma Richmond*

After losing their unborn baby, Sarah and Jed also lose the reason for their marriage. After weeks of awkward tolerance, one of them has to reach out, but who will it be? Can they reveal their true feelings and begin a real marriage?

### THE BABY ARRANGEMENT *by Moyra Tarling*

Faith had agreed to care for her identical twin's baby, and when Jared, the baby's father, arrived to claim him she found herself masquerading as Jared's wife! Although attracted to him, Faith couldn't give in to her feelings while she was living a lie...

### HUSBAND FOUND *by Martha Shields*

Rafe had been searching for his past—yet never expected to find a long-lost wife! And while Rafe was starting to remember her, Kate could not forget that he'd left her, and their unborn son, when they'd needed him most!

### A MISTRESS WORTH MARRYING *by Kay Thorpe*

A year ago Nicole had been seduced by Venezuelan millionaire, Marcos Peraza. When he proposed she had accepted—but that was before he discovered her deception. Now Nicole was back, Marcos was determined to get his revenge...

## *Available from 2nd June 2000*

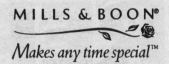

# MILLS & BOON®

*Makes any time special*™

# COMING SOON

## St. Elizabeth's Children's Hospital

A limited collection of 12 books. Where affairs of the heart are entwined with the everyday dealings of this warm and friendly children's hospital.

**Book 1**
**A Winter Bride by Meredith Webber**
**Published 5th May**

*Available at branches of WH Smith, Tesco,*
*Martins, RS McCall, Forbuoys, Borders, Easons,*
*Volume One/James Thin and most good paperback bookshops*

## 4 Books
### and a surprise gift!

We would like to take this opportunity to thank you for reading this Mills & Boon® book by offering you the chance to take FOUR more specially selected titles from the Presents...™ series absolutely FREE! We're also making this offer to introduce you to the benefits of the Reader Service™ —

- ★ FREE home delivery
- ★ FREE gifts and competitions
- ★ FREE monthly Newsletter
- ★ Books available before they're in the shops
- ★ Exclusive Reader Service discounts

Accepting these FREE books and gift places you under no obligation to buy; you may cancel at any time, even after receiving your free shipment. Simply complete your details below and return the entire page to the address below. *You don't even need a stamp!*

**YES!** Please send me 4 free Presents...™ books and a surprise gift. I understand that unless you hear from me, I will receive 6 superb new titles every month for just £2.40 each, postage and packing free. I am under no obligation to purchase any books and may cancel my subscription at any time. The free books and gift will be mine to keep in any case.

POEB

Ms/Mrs/Miss/Mr ........................................Initials ................................
BLOCK CAPITALS PLEASE

Surname ..............................................................................................

Address ...............................................................................................

.............................................................................................................

..................................................................Postcode .........................

**Send this whole page to:**
**UK: The Reader Service, FREEPOST CN81, Croydon, CR9 3WZ**
**EIRE: The Reader Service, PO Box 4546, Kilcock, County Kildare (stamp required)**